YOU'RE ON!

Shelby's lips curled in a confident grin. "How's she going to beat me at anything when she can't even get the right tack on her horse?"

Ashleigh knew she should keep quiet, but the insults stung. "I'll beat you in any event you want!" she hollered at Shelby's retreating form.

There was no reaction for a few moments, and Ashleigh wondered if the girl had heard her. After her horse took a few more strides, Shelby turned in her saddle and smiled sweetly.

"You're on!" the blond girl said, grinning confidently.

Ashleigh felt her stomach do a flip-flop as she realized what she had just done.

She had just issued a challenge that she wasn't at all sure she could win.

Collect all the books in the Thoroughbred series

Collect all the books in the Ashleigh series

---

* coming soon

THOROUGHBRED

Ashleigh

ASHLEIGH'S WESTERN CHALLENGE

CREATED BY

JOANNA CAMPBELL

WRITTEN BY

CHRIS PLATT

HarperEntertainment
An Imprint of HarperCollinsPublishers

HarperEntertainment
An Imprint of HarperCollins*Publishers*
10 East 53rd Street, New York, NY 10022-5299

 Produced by 17th Street Productions,
an Alloy Online, Inc., company

HarperCollins books are available at special quantity discounts for
bulk purchases for sales promotions, premiums, or fund-raising. For
information please call or write: Special Markets Department, HarperCollins
Publishers Inc., 10 East 53rd Street, New York, NY 10022-5299.
Telephone: (212) 207-7528. Fax: (212) 207-7222.

ISBN 0-06-009145-2

HarperCollins®, ■®, and HarperEntertainment™ are trademarks of
HarperCollins Publishers Inc.

Cover art © 2002 by 17th Street Productions,
an Alloy Online, Inc., company

First printing: November 2002

Printed in the United States of America

Visit HarperEntertainment on the World Wide Web at
www.harpercollins.com

❖ 10 9 8 7 6 5 4 3 2 1

1

"Remember this one?" eleven-year-old Ashleigh Griffen asked her older sister, Caroline, as she held up a glossy photograph from their family album.

Caroline looked up and lifted her long blond hair off her neck to catch the cooling breeze coming from the bedroom window. "I can't believe Kaitlin could fit all of those grapes in her mouth without choking," she said, chuckling. "She looks like a chipmunk in that picture."

Ashleigh grinned and flipped to the next photo, which also showed their cousins, the Gilberts. There was Kaitlin and her brother, Troy, and their parents, Jim and Linda. They had come from Nevada to Kentucky to visit during spring break. Everyone had enjoyed the visit, and it had been difficult to see them go when the week was over.

"Just think, Ash," Caroline said as she walked to the window and opened it all the way. "School will be out in another couple of days, and then you'll be on your way to Nevada to visit our cousins." She sat down on the end of Ashleigh's bed and fingered the airline ticket that lay on the dresser. "I wish I were the one going out west to visit," she said wistfully. "But you're the same age as Kaitlin, and since they live on a horse ranch, I guess it makes more sense that you go."

Ashleigh stared at the photo of Kaitlin. Her cousin had the same long dark hair that Ashleigh had, and they were about the same height. The Gilberts were on her father's side of the family. Both Ashleigh and her father had dark hair. Her mother, Caroline, and her five-year-old brother, Rory, were all blond.

Ashleigh picked up the letter that Kaitlin had sent her just the week before. The letter talked about the trouble her cousin was having with her favorite race-horse and how worried she was that he wouldn't do well in his first race. If the horse didn't seem to have the potential to be a champion, the Gilberts might not be able to keep him. Kaitlin really loved this horse. She needed Ashleigh's help.

"Hey, daydreamer," Caroline said as she picked up a pile of horse magazines and plopped them on Ash-leigh's bed. "I'm sure I'll miss you while you're gone, Ash. But it's going to be nice having the room all to myself," she said with a mischievous grin. "Especially when it'll be free of smelly boots and all these magazines you've got piled everywhere."

Ashleigh put the photo album away and snatched up the magazines, stuffing them under her bed. "Make sure you don't throw any of these away," she warned. "There are some good riding articles that I haven't gotten to yet."

"Just make sure they're put away before you go, and you won't have to worry about it," Caroline said as she picked up one of her movie star magazines and sat cross-legged on her bed.

Ashleigh stuck her tongue out at Caroline when she wasn't looking. There were some things that she wasn't going to miss when she went on vacation. Being bossed around by her older sister was one of them.

She grabbed her riding boots and headed for the door. "Don't forget that you've got to come down to the barn when I get back from my ride so that I can show you what we're doing with the foals."

Caroline nodded and waved her off without taking her eyes from the magazine's glossy pages.

Ashleigh frowned as she pulled the door closed behind her. Caroline didn't seem to be taking her new duties very seriously. Once Ashleigh was gone, it would be up to Caroline to help her parents work with the new foals. Although Caroline had barn chores to do just like the rest of the Griffen family, she wasn't into horses like everyone else. She wasn't good at handling them. Ashleigh hoped her sister wouldn't get hurt or do anything that would cause problems with the foals.

She slipped on her riding boots and grabbed an apple from the bowl on the kitchen counter, then ran out the door of the two-story white farmhouse to gather her horse from the pasture. Mona would be arriving soon, and she didn't want to make her friend wait.

Ashleigh climbed the white board fence that lined the broodmare pasture and whistled for Stardust. She had turned the little chestnut mare out into the pasture with Edgardale's mares and foals because Stardust enjoyed frolicking with the little ones. At the sound of the whistle, Stardust raised her head from the rich Kentucky bluegrass and whinnied a welcome before trotting over to the fence.

Ashleigh held the apple out to Stardust's soft muzzle, laughing when the mare took the entire apple into her mouth. "You can't eat it like that," Ashleigh admonished as she climbed down from the four-board fence and buckled on Stardust's halter. "You're supposed to take small bites, not be a pig."

Ashleigh giggled as she watched the mare work the apple around inside her mouth, trying to get it between her back teeth to crunch it. Finally the mare spit it out onto the grass and then took a proper bite. Ashleigh waited until Stardust was done with the apple, then led her toward Edgardale's large brown barn, where she would snap her into the crossties and saddle her.

Elaine Griffen popped her head out of the stall she was cleaning when Ashleigh entered the barn. She brushed her hair off her damp forehead and set the pitchfork aside. "Don't be gone long today, Ash," she warned as she moved the wheelbarrow on to the next stall. "We've got a lot of work to do with Caroline tonight."

Ashleigh nodded as she gathered her tack and the grooming kit. Stardust sighed and cocked a back foot as Ashleigh ran the rubber currycomb over her glistening coat and followed up with the soft brush. When she had finished picking the mare's feet, she set the saddle pad in place and hefted her new English saddle into place.

Ashleigh smiled as she ran her hands over the rich leather of the Robbie Ward saddle. She had competed for it in the spring. Her friend Mona had actually gone on to win the saddle, but she had given it to Ashleigh as a token of how much their friendship meant.

She reached under Stardust's belly and grabbed the cinch, frowning when she had to pull extra hard to get it to reach its normal hole. She wondered if Rory had been playing with her saddle, trying to make it fit his Shetland-Welsh cross, Moe.

Ashleigh walked to the other side to check the fastenings. She lifted the flap and frowned again. The cinch was set at the exact same place as it always was.

"I thought you were looking a little chubby," Ashleigh said as she ran a hand down the little chestnut's long white blaze. "I'd better talk to Mom and Dad about cutting back on your feed. You're not going to be getting much riding while I'm gone. I don't want you to get too fat."

Ashleigh let the cinch down a notch on the far side and tried once again to fasten it under the mare's belly. This time it reached. She patted the mare on the neck and grinned. "Big-time diet while I'm gone, girl." She cocked her head when she heard the *clip clop* beat of Frisky's hooves as Mona rode her bay Thoroughbred mare up Edgardale's long gravel driveway. She quickly bridled Stardust and reached for her riding helmet, then led the mare out of the barn to mount up.

"We've got to take a short ride today," Ashleigh said as she watched Frisky lift her four white-stockinged feet high into the air as she nickered excitedly to Stardust.

Mona pulled the mare to a halt and brushed her dark hair from her eyes as she grinned. "You wouldn't know we'd just been riding together two days ago," she said in amusement. "Frisky acts like she hasn't seen Stardust in ages."

Ashleigh settled in the saddle and turned Stardust toward the trails. "They're best friends, just like we are," she said with a grin.

"Best friends forever!" Mona said, but the smile quickly slipped from her face.

Ashleigh slowed Stardust and waited for Mona to catch up to her. "What's the matter? You look sad all of a sudden," she observed.

Mona dropped her chin and nodded. "I'm just really going to miss you, Ash," she said with a quiver in her voice. "You've never been gone as long as you're going to be this time."

Ashleigh took a deep breath, feeling kind of queasy in her stomach. "I'm really excited about going, but kind of scared, too," she admitted. "I'm going to be gone for six weeks of the summer, and I'm going to miss a lot of fun things here at home." She rode in silence for several moments, wrestling with her thoughts. "Sometimes I think that maybe I should just stay home."

Mona's head snapped around to stare at Ashleigh. "You can't be serious, Ash!"

Ashleigh shrugged. "My ticket's already been bought. I know I have to go," she said. "But then I think about the new foals, and how much of their schooling I'm going to miss, and all of the fun rides and things we'd get to do if I were home . . ."

Mona shook the tips of her reins at Ashleigh. "You'd better chase those thoughts right out of your head, Ash," she warned. "There's going to be lots of fun stuff to do in Nevada with your cousins. Just think," she said as a big smile crept over her face, "you're going to be able to see *real wild horses!* And there will be rodeos and rides through the desert." She sighed. "You and Kaitlin are going to have so much fun, you'll forget all about missing us back here."

Ashleigh looked doubtful. "I'm going to miss all of you terribly. But you're right, Mona. This vacation is going to be awesome!"

Mona bumped Frisky into a trot as they headed across the large meadow. "Just send lots of postcards, and don't forget to call every once in a while."

Ashleigh asked Stardust for a canter and sailed past her friend. She lifted her face to the sunshine and breathed in the strong green scent of spring as she galloped over the rich Kentucky bluegrass. The oak, maple, and Bradford pear trees were in full leaf, and pines stood tall against the cloudless blue sky. She wondered what it would be like in Nevada. Kaitlin said they lived in the high desert, but that wasn't the same as Death Valley's barren landscape, which Ashleigh had seen in pictures. In less than a week she would find out.

"Catch us if you can!" Mona hollered as she raced past on Frisky.

Frisky was pure Thoroughbred, and Stardust was only half. Ashleigh knew her little mare didn't have enough speed to beat Frisky, but Mona always slowed down enough to let them catch up.

The girls laughed as they raced around the large pasture with the wind whipping their cheeks and stinging their eyes. When the horses began to tire, they allowed them to drop down to a walk and spent several minutes cooling them out before letting them lower their heads to crop the sweet spring grass.

Ashleigh glanced at her watch. "I wish I had more time to ride. Stardust needs more of a workout. She's getting so fat, I had to let the saddle out a notch on the other side."

Mona tipped her head and studied the chestnut. "She does look like she's put on a few pounds," she agreed.

"I'm going to talk to my parents about cutting back on her feed. But with nobody to ride her while I'm gone, I'm afraid she's really going to be huge by the time I get back from vacation."

"I could ride Stardust for you while you're in Nevada," Mona volunteered.

Ashleigh's head popped up. "Would you?" she asked excitedly. "That would be really great!"

"Sure," Mona said. "This should be a fun vacation for you, Ash. I don't want you to worry about things back at Edgardale. I'll keep your mare in shape until you get home."

Ashleigh smiled her thanks. Mona was right. This was going to be a great vacation, and she was going to have a lot of fun. She pulled Stardust's head up and turned toward home. One of her worries had been taken care of. Now all she had to do was get Caroline ready to school the foals.

Jonas, Edgardale's only hired hand, and Ashleigh's parents were just bringing in the broodmares and foals when Ashleigh trotted up to the barn.

"Caroline's out back in the small paddock with Georgina and her filly. She's ready to start work," Mrs. Griffen said with a knowing smile.

Mr. Griffen handed Ashleigh a foal halter with a long lead rope attached. "Have patience with your sister, Ash," he warned. "You know Caroline isn't as enthusiastic about working with the horses as you and Rory are."

"I know, Dad." Ashleigh led Stardust to the barn to unsaddle her.

Jonas had just finished putting Althea and her colt into their stall when she entered the aisle. The old groom lifted his hat from his graying hair and indicated the crossties. "Just snap that mare into the ties and I'll take care of her. You don't want to keep your sister waiting too long."

Ashleigh removed Stardust's bridle and pulled her halter over her head. "Jonas?" she said.

Jonas hung Althea's halter outside the stall door and turned around. "Yes?"

Ashleigh ran her hands over Stardust's ribs, feeling the extra layer of fat that had recently appeared. "Stardust is starting to gain weight," she said. "Could you help my parents watch her while I'm gone and make sure she doesn't get any fatter?"

Jonas looked the mare over with a critical eye. "She does seem to be picking up a few more pounds," he observed. "I'll cut back some on her hay and grain rations."

Ashleigh thanked the old man and then went to find Caroline. Her sister was in the pen with My Georgina and her chestnut colt. Rudi, as Ashleigh liked to call the big colt with the rude attitude, was chewing on Caroline's shirt.

Caroline batted at the colt as she backed away. "Make him stop it, Ash," she hollered.

Ashleigh stifled a laugh and reached for Rudi. The

crafty colt twisted his lips and snagged her watchband as she buckled the halter over his elegant head. "No!" she said sternly as she gave his muzzle a warning tap. Rudi stopped and stared at her as though deciding whether he wanted to risk getting his nose swatted again.

Ashleigh handed the lead rope to Caroline. "*You* need to make him stop," she said. "No horse will respect you if you don't make it mind."

Rudi took a step toward Caroline and shoved his muzzle into her middle, getting ready to grab another mouthful of shirt.

"Yuck!" Caroline said as she backed out of reach of Rudi's wiggling lips and stared at her dirt-smudged shirt. "I don't want his respect," she said in an aggravated tone. "I just want him to stop slobbering on me."

Ashleigh rolled her eyes as she reached out to stop the young foal from nibbling on Caroline again. "Caro," Ashleigh said with as much patience as she could muster, "you live on this farm, too. I know you don't like working with the horses, but some of what you've seen and helped with has to have sunk into your head. You know you've got to have a horse's respect or it'll do as it pleases." She gave a short jerk on the lead rope to get Rudi's attention away from Caroline's shirt. "And when a horse does as it pleases, it's usually not something that will be pleasing to you."

Caroline huffed and took the lead rope that Ashleigh handed back to her.

"I'm going to lead Georgina," Ashleigh said. "Run the rope behind Rudi's hindquarters like I showed you, and you can walk him right beside us." She waited for Caroline to get the colt started, then she turned and asked Georgina to walk at a slow pace. Rudi and Caroline followed along behind.

They made one lap of the small pen, and Ashleigh was about to comment on how well Caroline and Rudi were doing when she heard a cry of distress from her sister. Ashleigh spun around to see Rudi rearing high into the air. Caroline set herself hard against the rope, and the colt touched down and then reared even higher as he shook his head to free himself from the constant pressure across the noseband of his halter.

"Give him some line!" Ashleigh cried. "You're pulling too hard on his nose. He's going to flip over backward!" Ashleigh rushed in and grabbed the lead rope from her frightened sister.

Rudi touched down and bolted forward to get to his mother's side, but Ashleigh was in the way. Ashleigh felt the hard impact as the young colt slammed into her, snapping her around before she fell to the ground in a heap.

The mare and foal took off to the other side of the pen as Caroline rushed to Ashleigh and knelt in the dirt beside her. "Are you okay, Ash?" she cried as she brushed the dirt from Ashleigh's clothes.

Ashleigh lay on the ground, waiting for the waves of pain to subside and for her breath to return. She sat up slowly and winced at the pain in her lower left leg. She bit her lip to keep from crying out, willing the ache to go away. She *couldn't* be hurt. Not now! If she was seriously injured, her parents wouldn't let her go to visit her cousins. She *had* to be okay—her summer vacation depended on it!

2

"What happened?" Mr. Griffen hollered as he ran from the barn toward the two girls. Mrs. Griffen was close on his heels.

Caroline leaned over Ashleigh, her face pinched with worry. "It's all my fault," she cried. "I couldn't control that stupid colt, and Ash got hurt when she tried to help me."

Ashleigh tried to give her sister a reassuring smile, but at the moment her whole body was pulsing with pain, and she wasn't sure that she *would* be okay. She tried to take a deep breath, but that sent sharp pain shooting across her midsection. She closed her eyes and grimaced. Her plane was leaving in three days. If she wasn't on it, she'd miss out on a great adventure.

"Is anything broken, Ash?" her mother asked as she bent to feel her daughter's arms and legs.

Ashleigh lay there in a daze, trying to figure out what pained her most, but at the moment everything hurt equally. "Give me just a minute," she said, trying to gather the strength to sit up. After a few moments some of the pain subsided, and she rolled into a sitting position.

"Be careful," Mr. Griffen warned. "If you've broken anything, we don't want to make it worse."

Ashleigh dusted the dirt off her shirt and looked around at the concerned faces of her family. "I think I'm all right," she said. "Nothing feels like it's broken—just badly bruised."

Mrs. Griffen gave her a hand up. "I think we should take you to the doctor just to be safe," she said as Ashleigh got to her feet.

Ashleigh gingerly walked a few steps, working her muscles to get the kinks out. "I think I just need to stretch a little," she said as she walked over to where Rudi stood nursing from his dam. She grabbed his lead rope and pulled him away from his mother.

"I think you've done enough for today," Mr. Griffen said as he reached out to take the colt from Ashleigh.

Ashleigh shook her head. "Rudi needs to know that he can't get away with this, and I need to walk a little. Caro, could you please lead Georgina?"

Together Ashleigh and Caroline led the horses around the small pen several times. Rudi tried to rear again, but Ashleigh kept a firm hand on him. When he seemed to be getting the knack of it, she traded horses with Caroline. After a few more good rounds they turned the horses loose.

Ashleigh stretched and gave her parents a smile. "I'm all right," she reassured them. "Just sore. I'll need an extra soak in the tub tonight."

Mrs. Griffen gave her a doubtful look. "You're not just pretending to be fine so we won't cancel your trip to visit your cousins, are you, Ash?"

Ashleigh shook her head, but deep down she knew that her mother was partly right. Outside of broken boncs, nothing was going to stop her from her western vacation—not even the fact that she now felt as though she'd been run over by a herd of horses. She looked from her mother to her father. They wouldn't stop her from going because of a small accident, would they?

Mrs. Griffen put her arm around Ashleigh's shoulders and steered her through the gate. "Why don't you go up to the house and start the bathwater," she suggested. "I'll help Caroline put away these horses. After dinner I'll help you choose your clothes for the trip."

A slow smile spread across Ashleigh's face, and she breathed a big sigh of relief. They were going to let her go! She walked quickly to the house, trying to hide a slight limp where Rudi had stepped on her foot. She went straight to the bathroom and started the water in the tub, pouring in a liberal amount of bubble bath, and then went in search of clean clothes.

Several minutes later, as she soaked in the hot, sudsy water, Ashleigh made herself a promise to be extra careful for the next several days. School let out early on Friday, and her plane was departing only a few hours after that. All she had to do was stay out of trouble for three more days, and then she'd be on the vacation of a lifetime!

The final days of school raced past, and before Ashleigh knew it, she was standing in Stardust's stall with her arms thrown around the mare's neck, crying quietly into her soft mane as she breathed in the warm horse scent.

"It's okay, Ashleigh," Rory said as he peeked into the stall. "I'll take care of Stardust for you. I can even ride her if you want."

Ashleigh brushed away her tears and tousled her little brother's red-gold hair. "Thanks, buddy. I bet Stardust would be really happy if you'd come by once a day and give her some carrots."

"Can I ride her, too?" Rory asked hopefully.

Ashleigh gave Stardust one final hug and closed the stall door. She put her arm around her little brother and led him out of the barn to where the rest of the family waited in the old station wagon. Her bags were already loaded in the trunk. "Thanks for the offer, Rory, but Mom and Dad said you're still too little to ride Stardust without someone holding on to her. When I get home you and Moe can go on some rides with Mona and me, okay?"

Rory nodded happily and climbed into the backseat of the car, squishing up close to Caroline to make room for Ashleigh and her carry-on bag. Ashleigh had packed a few snacks for the flight, and plenty of horse magazines.

"Buckle up, everyone," Mr. Griffen said. "The next stop will be the airport."

Ashleigh watched the green fields and blooming flowers pass outside the car window as she listened to the others chat. Her heart was pounding with excitement, but she didn't feel like joining the conversation. Her stomach was doing flip-flops, and her hands were all sweaty. She was happy to be going to see her cousins, but there was so much she was leaving behind that she would miss. Part of her was tempted to ask her father to turn the car around and go home, but the sensible part of her knew that this was just a bad case of the jitters. Once she got on that airplane she'd be excited to get to Nevada.

She looked around the car at the faces of her family

members, and she felt a large lump form in her throat. She was going to miss them all.

"Here we are," Mr. Griffen said as he turned onto the road marked Departing Flights. "I'll let all of you off at the front door so you can get Ashleigh checked in while I park the car."

Ashleigh waited until the car had come to a stop at the curb, then unbuckled her seat belt and stepped out onto the sidewalk. She tilted her head to watch a large jet pass in the distance, its powerful engines growling as the plane climbed high into the blue Kentucky sky. She felt a surge of excitement ripple through her. In a short while that would be her plane taking off, and she would be heading for her vacation adventure.

Mrs. Griffen grabbed Ashleigh's bags from the back of the station wagon and put Caroline in charge of keeping an eye on Rory. The little boy was so excited to see all of the airplanes, he could hardly contain himself. He darted here and there, pointing out each jet that passed overhead or taxied in the distance. Caroline herded Rory into the airport lobby, and everyone got into the long line to check Ashleigh's bags.

Mr. Griffen showed up several minutes later and volunteered to buy ice cream for everyone to help pass the time in the long, boring line. After what seemed like forever to Ashleigh, they finally got her bags checked and made it to the security checkpoint, where she would meet the airline employee who would help her board the plane.

A light-haired woman with a kind smile stepped forward to greet the Griffens. "Hi, I'm Mrs. Cline. I'll be taking Ashleigh to her airplane and introducing her to the flight attendants," the woman said in a soft voice. "I'll give you folks a few minutes to say goodbye. Let me know when you're ready."

Ashleigh swallowed hard as everyone gathered around to give her a final hug. It would be six whole weeks before she would see any of them again. Rory started to cry, and Caroline's eyes misted over.

"I think I'm actually going to miss you, brat," Caroline said as she gave Ashleigh a big-sister hug.

Ashleigh breathed deep, trying not to shed any tears. "Just remember to leave my horse magazines alone," she joked as she returned her sister's hug. Next she bent down on one knee to say goodbye to Rory, making him promise not to feed too many carrots to Stardust while she was gone. Her father gave her a solid, reassuring hug, but her mother held on to her as though she didn't want to let go, and Ashleigh felt the first tear slip down her cheek.

"Come on, Elaine," Mr. Griffen said. "We don't want Ash to miss her plane. Let's let the airline folks do their job."

Ashleigh slung her carry-on bag over her shoulder

and wiped at the moisture in her eyes, then waved a final goodbye and went with Mrs. Cline to board the plane. Since she was a kid traveling alone, she was one of the first ones to be seated. Mrs. Cline made sure she was fastened into the seat properly and then introduced her to the flight attendant who would be serving in Ashleigh's area. Ashleigh immediately liked the perky brunette and felt herself relaxing as she settled down with a set of headphones that allowed her to listen to the control tower.

Ashleigh peered into the faces of the other travelers as they stepped onto the plane. She wondered where they were going and who was waiting for them at the end of the plane ride. That reminded her that she would soon see her cousins, and before long she was all excited again.

When everyone had boarded the plane, the captain's voice came over the speaker, telling them to prepare for departure. Ashleigh stared out the small window as the jet backed away from the terminal and taxied to the runway. The big plane traveled for several minutes and then made a slow turn onto the main runway. The aircraft paused for a moment while the engines revved, then surged forward, gaining speed as it rumbled down the airstrip.

Ashleigh gripped the armrest and pressed back into her seat as the plane lifted off, climbing high into the sky. She had flown only once before, when the Danworths had taken her family down to Florida to watch Aladdin's Treasure win a big stakes race. But that had been a small private jet. It wasn't anything like this big jetliner.

When the plane leveled off, Ashleigh leaned forward and looked out the small window at the landscape below. The land was flat with a few rolling hills, and everything was so green. She was amazed at how small the houses seemed.

After a while the stress of the day and the hum of the engines lulled her into a drowsy state. When a flight attendant offered her a pillow, Ashleigh gladly accepted it and tucked it between her head and the side of the airplane. Within moments she was asleep.

When Ashleigh woke for the dinner service two hours later, the landscape below had changed drastically. The green had been replaced with large areas of brown with small green fields scattered here and there. And there were huge mountains, the likes of which Ashleigh had never seen before except in photos. She sucked in her breath at the sight of the tall, craggy, snow-covered peaks.

By the time she was finished with her dinner of

roasted chicken and salad, the sun was setting. She wished that the daylight would last a little longer. She wanted to be able to see Nevada when she stepped off the plane.

Ashleigh sat back in her seat. It didn't really matter, she decided—she'd have the next six weeks to see as much of her cousins' home as she could. Kaitlin had promised her rides through the desert and into the mountains, plus rodeos, horse races, and swims in natural hot springs. She absolutely couldn't wait!

She glanced at her watch. They still had another forty-five minutes before they landed. She pulled out a magazine that Mona had given her just that morning when she came to say goodbye. It was full of facts about the state of Nevada. She was surprised to learn that although it wasn't very populous, Nevada was one of the fastest-growing states in the nation. And the area that she was visiting, just outside of Reno, only received an average of seven inches of rain in a year.

Ashleigh grinned. In Kentucky they could get that much rain in a few *days* if the storm was bad enough. It was no wonder the ground below seemed so brown. Seven inches of precipitation in one year wasn't enough to make the land green.

The jet made a slight turn, and Ashleigh noticed a difference in the pitch of the engines. A moment later the captain's voice came over the speakers, telling them that they were beginning their descent into Reno. The flight attendant stopped by to pick up the remaining trash and to check that everyone's seat belt was fastened. Ashleigh returned her magazine to her carry-on bag and stuffed it under the seat in front of her in preparation for landing.

Ten minutes later they were on the ground, and Ashleigh was met by another airline employee. Together they walked to the baggage claim area, where Ashleigh planned to meet her cousins.

Ashleigh could hear Kaitlin hollering before she actually saw the dark-haired girl cutting through the crowd and running toward her. Troy and Mr. and Mrs. Gilbert weaved their way behind her, struggling to keep up.

"Ashleigh, you're here!" Kaitlin reached out and gave Ashleigh a big hug, then grabbed her by the hand and dragged her back toward the rest of the family. Ashleigh received hugs from each of them, except for Troy, who looked embarrassed and stood scuffing the floor with the toe of his boot. Quietly he offered to take Ashleigh's carry-on bag.

As they caught each other up on all of their news, Ashleigh and her cousin strode over to the baggage carousel to collect Ashleigh's suitcases. Kaitlin talked nonstop about all the fun they were going to have and all of the plans she had made for the two of them.

"Tomorrow we'll get down to the barn first thing in the morning so I can introduce you to all the horses, and you can pick out a couple that you'd like to ride for your stay here," Kaitlin said.

Ashleigh pointed out a brown tweed bag that belonged to her, and Troy plucked it from the conveyer belt. "I get to pick out a *couple* of horses?" she asked. The other bag came down the belt, and Jim grabbed it. "How many horses do you have?"

Kaitlin shrugged. "We've got about twenty, but some of them are yearlings, and some of them have leg trouble from racing, so we're giving them a rest. But we've got lots of riding horses to choose from."

They moved toward the door marked Exit and stepped into the warm night. Ashleigh lifted her nose and breathed deeply. "Wow, it sure smells different out here. What's that strange smell?"

Kaitlin shrugged. "I'm so used to the way things smell that I don't really notice it much. It's probably the sagebrush that you're talking about. Northern Nevada has a lot of sage and bitterbrush. They've got a very distinctive smell."

Ashleigh nodded as she took another deep breath. "It smells really nice, like some of the herbs in my mom's garden."

Kaitlin opened the door of their extended-cab

pickup truck. "If you think this smells good, just wait until after we have a good rain."

Ashleigh climbed into the backseat of the truck and laughed. "From what I've read about Nevada, it doesn't sound like you get very much rain."

Kaitlin settled into the seat next to Ashleigh, making room for her brother. "You're right. We don't get a whole lot of rain, but just a little sprinkle and the desert smells like nothing you've ever imagined."

The truck pulled out of the parking lot and onto the road that led to the freeway.

"It's about a half-hour drive to our house," Jim said. "You must be tired, Ashleigh, with the time difference and all. It's three hours later out in Kentucky."

Linda gave her an understanding smile. "You girls can start fresh in the morning. Tonight you'll have just enough time to unpack before bedtime."

Ashleigh stared out of the truck's windows into the darkness beyond. She wished she could see the landscape. Was it as brown as the land she had seen from the air?

As she wondered what the morning would bring, the hum of the truck's engine and the heat of the summer night lulled Ashleigh into a stupor, and she felt her eyes growing heavy. Thirty minutes later she was jolted awake when the truck turned off the freeway and bumped down a dirt road. After a few minutes on the rough road, they pulled into a long driveway and parked in front of a small one-story house.

"This is it," Kaitlin said as she jumped out of the truck. "The barn's actually bigger than our house! The house is small, but it's the right size for us."

Ashleigh waited while Troy and his father gathered her bags, then she followed them into the house. She sat her carry-on down in the living room, taking in her surroundings. The house wasn't much different from the old farmhouse at Edgardale, except this one was much smaller.

Kaitlin motioned for her to follow, and Ashleigh walked down the hallway to the last bedroom on the left.

"This is my room," Kaitlin said as she pushed the door open. "We'll have to share a bed, but at least it's big enough."

Ashleigh smiled as she looked around the small, sparsely furnished room. There were horse posters covering the walls and win photos of the Gilberts' horses everywhere. She could see horse magazines that had been hastily stuffed under the bed, and a pair of cowboy boots stood in the corner.

She felt more at home seeing all the trappings of her own room right here in Kaitlin's. But later, as they turned out the lights and lay in the dark, whispering plans for the next day, Ashleigh thought about her family, friends, and horses, which were now two thousand miles away. A big, empty ache settled over her as she wondered whether a long stay had been the correct decision.

3

When a rooster crowed just outside the bedroom window, Ashleigh sat bolt upright in bed. She blinked hard as she stared around the room, feeling disoriented and unsure of her surroundings. Her heart beat wildly in her chest as she tried to figure out where she was.

"What's the matter, Ash?" Kaitlin said in a sleepy voice as she tugged at the covers Ashleigh had tossed to the foot of the bed.

Ashleigh blinked again, and her surroundings came into focus. She let out a sigh of relief as she realized why everything seemed so unfamiliar to her. She was in northern Nevada, and the first day of her vacation was about to begin.

"What time is it?" Kaitlin asked in a groggy voice.

"It's just after six," Ashleigh said. "The rooster is crowing."

Kaitlin rolled over and put her head under the covers. "See those rocks on the windowsill?" Her muffled voice came from under the light quilt. "If he crows again, open the window and toss some rocks in his direction to scare him off the fence."

"What?" Ashleigh said in surprise.

Kaitlin peeked her head out from the covers. "I don't mean *hit* him. Just scare him away. It's summer vacation and it's Saturday. My family sleeps in until seven-thirty. Go back to sleep for another hour, Ash. Then we'll have breakfast and go meet the horses."

Ashleigh lay back down and tried to sleep, but it was impossible. At Edgardale it was nine o'clock, and everyone would be busy cleaning stalls and working with the horses.

Kaitlin's slow, steady breathing told Ashleigh that her cousin had fallen back to sleep. She closed her eyes and thought about Edgardale. She hoped everyone remembered to keep Stardust on a diet and that Mona would be able to take her on a few long rides.

Ashleigh lost herself in thoughts of Edgardale and her friends Mona, Jamie, and Lynne. She was about to have another bout of homesickness when she heard her cousin stirring.

Kaitlin stretched and sat up in the bed. "I guess you didn't have to scare that silly rooster off his perch," she said with a grin.

Ashleigh looked at the rocks that lined the windowsill. "Does he do that *every* morning?"

Kaitlin swung her legs over the side of the bed and nodded. "But sometimes he does it on the other side of the house. It's not so loud when he crows over there."

Ashleigh grabbed a pair of jeans and a T-shirt out of her suitcase. It felt kind of cool at the moment, but the weather report she'd heard on the ride from the airport the night before had said that it was going to climb into the nineties.

Ashleigh finished dressing and followed Kaitlin downstairs. Jim and Troy were just putting on their boots when the girls entered the kitchen.

"Linda's out throwing the morning hay," Jim said. "We'll see you girls at the barn as soon as you're ready."

Ashleigh and Kaitlin gulped down a glass of orange juice, then ran out of the house to the horse pens. Ashleigh got no more than four steps out of the house when she noticed her surroundings.

"Whoa!" Ashleigh stopped in her tracks as she surveyed the area around her. This was nothing like home. Her cousins had a small patch of grass around their back steps and, from what she remembered of the previous night, another small yard in the front. But the rest of the property, including the barnyard, was all golden sand.

At the edge of the property, scraggly light green

bushes popped up everywhere. Above the somber colors of the land, the sky was a brilliant blue.

"What's the matter, Ash?" Kaitlin stopped and turned, waiting for Ashleigh to catch up.

"It looks so . . . different," she said for lack of a better word. "Everything is so brown."

Kaitlin laughed as she looped her arm through Ashleigh's and pulled her toward their old wooden barn. "Not *everything* is brown," she said. "It's just the shock of seeing the high desert for the first time when you come from a land of green." She took a deep breath of the fresh desert air. "We're going to ride in some really great places, Ashleigh. And you'll see things you'll never see in Kentucky." She gave her cousin a wide grin. "You'll learn to love this place in the six weeks you're here."

Ashleigh tried to look excited. But it didn't look as though there was much to love in the landscape, except maybe the mountains. Every time she looked at the snow-capped peaks, it took her breath away.

Kaitlin opened the door to the barn. "This is Ranger," she said, pointing to the small bay horse sticking his head over the stall door. "He's mine to race," she said proudly as she lovingly rubbed the small white star in the center of the gelding's forehead. "Three years ago my parents gave both my brother and me a colt to raise and race. Whatever our horses win in purse money, we get to put in our savings account for college."

"What a cool idea!" Ashleigh said. "I wish my parents would let me do that. I've always wanted to keep one of our foals and train it to race."

"I'd like to go to veterinary college," Kaitlin said with pride. "So I hope Ranger does really well at the track. My parents will never be able to afford to send me to an expensive school otherwise." She rubbed Ranger's head and frowned. "I'm worried, though," Kaitlin admitted. "Like I told you in my letter, Ranger doesn't seem to be too interested in training right now. I just hope he'll snap out of it before long."

Ashleigh extended her hand for the bay to sniff. When he nuzzled her hand, she stepped closer and gave him a good scratch between the big bones under his jaw. Ranger extended his head, telling her he wanted more. "When's his first race?" she asked.

"Ranger does a timed workout tomorrow, and he'll run his first race next week," Kaitlin said as she grabbed the feed buckets and began mixing the morning grain for the racers.

Ashleigh helped her cousin carry the buckets to the other five racers in the barn. "Is it a stakes race?" she asked.

Kaitlin gave a snort of laughter. "Yeah, right!" she scoffed. "Like my family could afford to buy or breed a stakes horse. You've been hanging around those rich people at the big tracks for too long, Ash. There are a lot of people in horse racing who own twenty-five-hundred-dollar claimers. That's what Ranger is running in."

"Our horses aren't all big stakes winners," Ashleigh said in defense of her family, though she wasn't quite sure what she was defending them against.

"I'm not trying to hurt your feelings, Ash," Kaitlin said in apology. "It's just that there's a big difference between the kinds of racetracks you're used to and the small bush tracks where we run our horses."

Ashleigh pursed her lips in thought. "But what kind of a win purse are you racing for if the claiming price is so cheap?"

Kaitlin shrugged. "The purses are always lower than the claiming price, and the winner only gets sixty percent of that." She stacked the empty buckets and motioned for Ashleigh to follow her outside. "The worst part is that there are only a couple of racetracks in Nevada, and they only race a couple of weeks out of the year. None of the tracks here are recognized by the *Daily Racing Form*. The only places we have to run our horses are bush tracks. Mostly we haul into northern California to race. There are quite a few bush and recognized tracks there."

Ashleigh laughed. "How did bush tracks get that name?"

Kaitlin shrugged. "I suppose it's because they're

out-of-the-way tracks that aren't recognized in the big leagues. Don't they call minor-league baseball teams the bush leagues?"

"I think you're right," Ashleigh said. "I can't wait to see the track."

Kaitlin snickered. "You're not missing much, Ash."

They walked toward a large fenced area that had no grass growing in it. There were five horses standing at the fence nickering for their morning feed. "What are the bush tracks like?"

Kaitlin grabbed an armload of grass hay that her mother had left for her and waited for Ashleigh to open the gate. "They're usually small. Some of them are only a half mile around," she explained. "They use the same rules as the big racetracks, but they're a little more lax. There's not as much money involved in the purses and upkeep of the grounds. The barns aren't always the greatest." She tossed the hay into several large feeder tires next to the fence. "You'll get to see one next week when Ranger races."

"I thought you said you have to go all the way to California to race," Ashleigh commented.

Kaitlin smiled. "We're less than fifty miles from the California border, Ash. It's not like it's a ten-hour drive to get there. The track we're racing at this time is about two hours away."

"I can't wait!" Ashleigh said as she climbed the four-board fence to sit on the top rail. "So, who are these beauties?" she asked, watching the horses move from feeder to feeder until they settled in the right pecking order.

Kaitlin joined Ashleigh on the fence. "Those two bay quarter horses are my dad's and my brother's roping horses," she said as she pointed at two geldings eating out of the same feeder. "The chestnut belongs to my mom. She lets me use him whenever I want. The buckskin is Tony. He's mine, but he's getting pretty old and I don't ride him very hard anymore," she explained. "The black-and-white paint mare and the gray Arabian mare are family horses." She turned to Ashleigh. "We'll be doing a lot of riding while you're here, so you need to pick two horses that you'd like to be yours for your stay."

Ashleigh smiled and turned her attention back to the horses. The stocky quarter horses would be fun to try. She'd never ridden one before. But they belonged to Jim and Troy, and she knew that they did a lot of roping at local arenas.

The chestnut mare was cute, but Kaitlin and her mother would be riding him. And the buckskin was too old for much riding. "I'll pick the paint and the Arab," she said.

Kaitlin nodded her approval of the paint. "The paint's a great choice," she said. "But that Arabian mare doesn't get ridden much because she's pretty tough to ride."

Ashleigh arched her brows in curiosity. "What does she do?" she asked.

Kaitlin brushed her long dark hair over her shoulders and smirked. "The question is, what *doesn't* she do?" she said with a laugh. "Her name is Ariel, and she can go farther than any horse we've got. But she's spooky, and she's a high-headed thing with a lot of spunk."

"Can't you longe her for a few minutes before you get on her?" Ashleigh asked. "That always helps with Stardust when she's feeling good." But even before Ashleigh finished speaking, she saw the knowing smile on her cousin's face.

"I guess you've never ridden an Arabian before." Kaitlin climbed down from the fence and walked over to the flea-bitten gray, giving her an affectionate pat. "These horses are used to competing in fifty-and hundred-mile races. You can't tire them out with a little bit of longeing," she said. "If Ariel gets her tail up over her back, you're going to have a very long, trying ride."

Ashleigh looked at the little mare, who wasn't even fifteen hands high. Ariel seemed so mellow as she stood there quietly eating from the feeder. But Ashleigh decided to take Kaitlin's advice. She'd keep her wits about her when she rode the mare.

"Come on," Kaitlin said. "Let's go eat breakfast. By the time we get done eating and look for a saddle that fits you, the horses will be ready to go for a ride."

Ashleigh climbed down from the fence and followed her cousin to the house. The smell of pancakes wafted toward them when they walked through the door. It made her stomach growl.

"I hope you're hungry," Linda said as she flipped a golden brown pancake. "You girls can wash your hands in the kitchen sink and sit down at the table."

Troy hurried into the kitchen with a track helmet on his head. He pulled out a chair and sat next to Ashleigh. "I hope you saved some for me."

Linda set a plate full of steaming pancakes on the table. She gave her son a warning glance, and Troy quickly slipped the helmet from his head and set it on the floor at his feet.

"Sorry, Mom," the teenager said. "I'm running a little late this morning. Dad's got three horses to work, and I'm supposed to be at the training track in ten minutes." Despite his hurry, he offered the pancakes to his sister and Ashleigh before he piled his plate high and poured on a liberal dose of syrup.

Kaitlin looked at her brother's heaped plate. "You'll never be a jockey if you keep eating like that."

Troy crammed a huge bite into his mouth, and a dribble of syrup made its way down his chin. He chewed the mouthful, then turned to his sister. "I'm already too big to be a jockey. I'll settle for galloping at one of the big California tracks for a few years. Then, when I'm older, I'll be a trainer like Dad."

"Ashleigh's going to be a jockey someday," Kaitlin said.

Tory forked another large bite of pancakes into his mouth and gave Ashleigh a teasing wink. "She looks like she's going to be the right size, but that's a pretty big stack of pancakes she's got there. If you keep eating like me, Ash, you'll outgrow the job."

Ashleigh grinned. She knew she wouldn't be too big for the job. Maybe someday she'd go to California and ride some of Troy's horses once he got to be a big trainer.

They finished breakfast and went back to the barn.

"Don't you want to see Troy gallop?" Ashleigh asked, anxious to get a peek at their training track.

Kaitlin shook her head. "We'll watch him work Ranger tomorrow. Today I want to introduce you to the Nevada wilderness. Let's go saddle the horses."

Ashleigh followed Kaitlin into the tack room. There were several saddles, large and small, sitting on saddle racks.

"How about this one?" Kaitlin said as she pointed to a black western saddle. "It looks about your size."

Ashleigh eyed the saddle dubiously. She lifted it

from the rack. It weighed more than twice what her English saddle did. And it seemed rather bulky, with all its big leather panels. "Do you have an English saddle?" she asked nervously.

Kaitlin looked up in surprise. "These are western horses, Ash. They're neck-reined and everything. Why would you want to ride in an English saddle?"

Ashleigh shrugged. "I'm just used to that kind," she said. "That's all I ever ride in. I think I'd feel more confident riding in something I'm used to. Especially when I'm riding a new horse in a new place."

Kaitlin scratched her head as she glanced about the tack room. "We used to have a beat-up one lying around here a few years back, but nobody ever used it." She dug under a pile of dusty saddle pads that had been tossed into the corner. "Here it is." She held up the old English saddle in triumph. "I know it's not as pretty as the one Mona gave you, but it looks like it has all the parts."

Ashleigh took the saddle and the paint mare's bridle from Kaitlin and headed for the big pen beside the barn. "What's the paint's name?" she asked as she set the equipment on the fence.

"Her name's Flash," Kaitlin said. "My mother named her. The white pattern on her neck looks like a flash of lightning."

"I like that," Ashleigh said. "She's beautiful. The

name fits her because she looks very flashy." She waited for Kaitlin to halter the paint mare and tie her to the fence, then she took one of the body brushes and began brushing the mare's shiny coat.

When Ashleigh went to slip the bit into Flash's mouth, she paused to study it. Instead of the broken snaffle that Stardust wore, this bit was a solid piece with a big curve in the middle. "I always thought these bits were cruel," she said to her cousin.

"They can be in the wrong hands," Kaitlin replied. "But since most western horses move from the touch of the rein on their neck and the leg pressure on their sides, there's really not supposed to be much pressure on that bit. A good western horse should move on a loose rein."

Ashleigh gently bridled the mare, making a mental note to go very easy on the reins. This was going to be so different from riding English horses, where a rider *wanted* contact with the horse's mouth.

When the horses were saddled, they led them from the pen and mounted up.

"Most of what you see out here is BLM land," Kaitlin explained as she headed for a sandy trail between two bushes. "*BLM* stands for Bureau of Land Management. The BLM and the National Forest Service manage it," she said. "And we get to ride on it anytime we want!" She bumped her old buckskin into a trot.

Ashleigh posted in time to Flash's gait, but she discovered that the mare was so smooth, she could actually sit the trot. They passed rather close to one of the scraggly bushes at the trail's edge, and Ashleigh felt it scratch through her pant leg. "Ouch!" she said as she pulled her leg tighter to Flash's side. The mare felt the pressure and immediately moved over. Ashleigh smiled at the horse's quick response. She hadn't intended to cue the mare over, but the horse had acted appropriately to the leg pressure. Ashleigh wished Stardust were this light.

"Hey, Kaitlin," she called to her cousin. "What kind of bushes are these?"

"That's sagebrush," she answered. "We smelled that last night, remember? It's probably the most abundant of all the brush out here." She pointed to a similar-looking bush that had small yellow blossoms blooming on it. "This is the other bush that gives Nevada that distinctive smell. Take a whiff when you go by," she said. "It's called bitterbrush, but the smell's not really that bad."

Ashleigh took a deep breath. "Mmm." She indicated another thorny-looking bush that had beautiful pink blossoms all over it. "What's that over there?" she asked.

"That's what we call desert peach brush." Kaitlin

gestured farther up the small hill they were approaching. "See that up there?"

Ashleigh shaded her eyes and saw a bush that looked the same but had lighter-colored flowers tinged with peach.

"That's the same desert peach bush. I'm not sure why they're different colors, but they can range from a pale pink or peach to a very dark shade of the same color." Kaitlin turned around in her saddle. "Just wait until we get to the other side of this hill," she said with a grin. "You told me earlier that there's not much color here besides brown. . . ."

Ashleigh leaned forward in the saddle as Flash dug in and trotted up the hillside. When they reached the top, Ashleigh pulled the mare to a stop and sat in awe at the sight before her. The entire side of the hill that faced the morning sun was covered with bright yellow flowers that looked like big daisies. "Wow!" she said, stunned. "What are those?"

Kaitlin beamed proudly as if it were her own private garden. "Those are balsamroot flowers. And the pretty purple flowers that look like lilacs growing out of the ground are lupines."

"This is totally awesome, Kaitlin," Ashleigh said as she stared at the beauty before her, trying to drink it all in with her eyes. "I never would have guessed there would be this kind of color out here. From the airplane, and even from the house, everything looks drab."

Kaitlin nodded in understanding. "A lot of people think the same thing when they first see this land. But if you take the time to go out into the high desert, you'll discover a whole lot of color and life out here." She smiled at Ashleigh. "Just wait until we find some Indian paintbrush!"

"What's that?" Ashleigh asked.

"It's a special flower," Kaitlin said. "They say that the seeds for an Indian paintbrush can germinate only if they first go through the digestive tract of a bird. They're kind of hard to find, but when you find them, there are usually several of them in one place. They're brilliant shades of red, and they look kind of like a bushy pipe cleaner."

Ashleigh scanned the valley below them, seeing more traces of color and the beautiful mountains that rose out of the ground. She spotted a large ranch that appeared to be about a half mile from her cousin's place. "Who owns that spread?" she asked, noting the instant frown that came to her cousin's face.

"That's the Jeffreys' ranch," Kaitlin said in a frosty tone. "Home to Miss Shelby Jeffrey, rodeo queen, barrel racer, professional snob, and the biggest brat at my school."

"That's a long list of impressive titles," Ashleigh said with a laugh. "I guess I'd better hope I never have to meet her."

Kaitlin scoffed. "I'm sure you'll run into her somewhere. We'll be going to the Reno Rodeo tomorrow. It's one of the richest rodeos in the west. Since Shelby's in the running to be this year's rodeo queen, she'll be riding her horse in the arena between events."

"I'll keep my distance for as long as I can," Ashleigh said as they rode on. But as it turned out, she wasn't able to keep that promise for more than a few hours. On the ride back to the Gilberts' small ranch, they ran across Shelby on the trail.

"Who's your new friend, Kaitlin?" Shelby asked as she pulled her golden palomino gelding to a halt, leaning forward in the saddle to straighten a few mane hairs that had fallen out of place.

Ashleigh noted that the girl's hair was almost the same color as the palomino's. It was long and wavy, and didn't seem to have any trouble staying combed—unlike Ashleigh's hair, which hung in her eyes and tangled in a wild array over her shoulders.

"This is my cousin, Ashleigh," Kaitlin said as she tried to walk her horse down the trail. But Shelby moved into the middle of the pathway, so Kaitlin was forced to stop.

"She looks kind of prissy sitting on top of that goofy

English saddle," Shelby said. "I bet she can't even rope." She gave Ashleigh a dismissive look.

Ashleigh bristled. The girl was talking about her as if she weren't even there. Why was she insulting her when she didn't even know her? It was true that Ashleigh didn't know anything about roping or barrel racing, but she could learn.

"Ashleigh's a much better horsewoman than you are, Shelby," Kaitlin said. "I'm sure she could beat you in any of those gymkhana events if she had a couple of weeks to practice."

Shelby's lips curled in a confident grin. "Yeah, right!" she snorted in disbelief. "How's she going to beat me at anything when she can't even get the right tack on her horse?" With that, the girl waved them off and headed down the trail.

Ashleigh couldn't believe she was being treated so badly when she had just been introduced. She knew she should keep quiet, but the insults stung, and before she knew it she was issuing a challenge to the snobby neighbor girl. "I'll beat you in any event you want!" she hollered at Shelby's retreating form.

There was no reaction for a few moments, and Ashleigh wondered if the girl had heard her. After her horse took a few more strides, Shelby turned in her saddle and smiled sweetly.

"You're on!" the blond girl said, grinning confidently.

Ashleigh felt her stomach do a flip-flop as she realized what she had just done.

She had just issued a challenge that she wasn't at all sure she could win.

4

Ashleigh pursed her lips, wondering what she was going to do now. She didn't know anything about barrel racing or roping. She didn't even know Shelby Jeffrey. What had possessed her to challenge the girl to a contest?

"Are you okay, Ash?" Kaitlin asked as she rode her horse next to Flash.

Ashleigh shrugged. "I'm not sure." She turned in the saddle to face her cousin. "I think I just made a big mistake."

Kaitlin grinned. "It was kind of crazy of you to challenge a rodeo queen to a sport she's really good at."

Ashleigh felt her stomach twist again. When would she ever learn to keep her big mouth shut? "Maybe I should just swallow my pride and ride after her to tell her the deal's off." She looked to Kaitlin for help.

Kaitlin furrowed her brow in thought and then

shook her head. "No, I don't think so." She moved her gelding down the path toward home. "This is doable, Ash," she said encouragingly. "At least the barrel-racing part. That mare you're riding runs better times than Shelby's horse. Her parents have tried to buy Flash several times. All you have to do is learn the barrel pattern and stay on, and I think you could beat her."

"Gee, thanks," Ashleigh said. She was aware Kaitlin hadn't meant to hurt her feelings, but her cousin's words stung nonetheless. Ashleigh knew she could do more than just hang on while the mare did all the work.

"Oh, stop it, Ash," Kaitlin admonished. "I'm just giving you a hard time. You're one of the best riders I know. I'm just trying to make the point that you *can* do this."

Ashleigh reined her mare in behind Kaitlin as the trail narrowed to go through the sagebrush. "What about roping? That looks really tough to me."

Kaitlin steered her horse around a big rock in the path. "That part might be a problem, Ash. I've been roping for years, and I'm still not that good at it."

"Great," Ashleigh said in dismay.

"We'll talk to Troy as soon as we get home. He's really good at roping. I'm sure he'd be happy to help."

"But what hope do I have when you've been doing it

for years and still aren't good at it, and I've only got a few weeks?" Ashleigh cried.

"Let's hope that you're a natural and you pick it up quickly," Kaitlin said with a smile. "There's our ranch." She pointed to the small house and barn in the distance. "Let's hurry. I've got to check Ranger's legs and make sure he's ready to work tomorrow."

Ashleigh perked up when her cousin started talking about horse racing. That was one area she felt totally comfortable with. But thoughts of competing with Shelby wouldn't go away. "When can we start my gymkhana lessons?" she asked. The sooner they got started, the better.

"We'll have to wait until Monday to start," Kaitlin said. "We've got a full day ahead of us tomorrow. Ranger works in the morning, and my parents are taking us to the Reno Rodeo at night."

Ashleigh rode the rest of the way in silence. She hated losing a day of practice, but maybe watching the professionals in the rodeo would give her some hints about how it was really done.

On Sunday morning Ashleigh was once again awakened by the rooster crowing outside their bedroom window. She put both feet over the side of the bed and opened the window. "Shoo!" she said as she made fluttering motions with her hands. The bantam cocked his head and stared at her for a moment, then made clucking noises that sounded suspiciously like a chuckle before jumping off the fence and strutting across the yard.

Ashleigh closed the window and lay back down. She and Kaitlin had stayed up long after the lights had gone out to make plans for this day. She was excited about going to the rodeo. She'd never been to a real one before. Ashleigh couldn't wait to see the bareback broncs and the bull riding.

As she imagined the fun they were going to have, she felt her eyelids grow heavy. She thought she'd only closed her eyes for a moment, but when she opened them again, it was seven-thirty and Kaitlin was getting dressed for the day.

"Come on, sleepyhead," Kaitlin said as she pulled a T-shirt over her head. "Let's eat breakfast and get out to the barn. Troy is down feeding the horses their morning grain. We've got to get Ranger brushed and saddled."

Ashleigh got out of bed and dressed quickly. As she was tucking her T-shirt into her jeans, she noticed several red drops on the blue shirt. "Oh, no!" she said. "I've got a nosebleed."

Kaitlin handed her several tissues. "Welcome to

Nevada, Ash. Most people who come to visit usually get a nosebleed or two in the first couple of days."

Ashleigh pinched her nose to help stop the bleeding. "Why is that?" she mumbled through the tissues.

"You come from a humid place, and it's very dry out here," Kaitlin explained. "We only have seven percent humidity. I bet your lips are chapped, too." She tossed Ashleigh some lip balm. "I'll get you something to help keep your nose from bleeding again. You'll get used to the dry weather in a few days." She brought Ashleigh some ointment from the medicine chest. "I'll see you downstairs in a few minutes."

Ashleigh cleaned up and changed her shirt. She continued to be amazed at how different Nevada was from Kentucky. But there was one thing that she was sure was the same—horse racing! Working with Thoroughbred racers was exciting no matter where you were. And Ranger was in the barn waiting to be saddled for his work.

She hurried to the kitchen to join Kaitlin for a breakfast of cold cereal and fresh strawberries. As Ashleigh spooned the fresh fruit and crunchy cereal into her mouth, she felt a little more at home. She ate this same thing many mornings back at Edgardale. Her mind wandered, and she wondered how Caroline was doing with the foals. She hoped Caro was being helpful to their parents.

Kaitlin finished her cereal and took her bowl to the sink, rinsing it before placing it in the dishwasher. "I can't wait to see Ranger work," she said. "Just think, Ash. Before the week is out, Ranger will run in his first race!"

Ashleigh placed her dish in the dishwasher and reached for her boots. "You're so lucky, Kate," she said as she tugged on her English riding boots. "I wish my parents would let me keep one of our foals to raise and race. It must be a lot of fun to watch a horse that you've raised from a baby race under your own colors." She followed Kaitlin out the back door to the barn.

"They don't always run under our colors," Kaitlin said. "If we haul to Oregon, the Oregon Racing Commission has their own color codes. Each post position has a certain color, and it's always the same all over the state."

Ashleigh was surprised. She was used to seeing all the varied racing silks of the big and small stables at home. "I guess that would make it easier to keep the post positions straight," she said.

They entered the barn, and Ranger nickered at the sound of his owner's voice. Kaitlin went to him and took his muzzle in her hands, planting a kiss on the tip of his nose. "You're going to burn up the track today, aren't you, boy?"

Ashleigh felt a pang of homesickness as she watched the loving exchange between Kaitlin and Ranger. She missed Stardust horribly. She hoped Mona was riding the little mare and that Rory remembered to give her some carrots each day.

Troy entered the barn and grabbed his helmet off the peg on the wall. "Quit babying that horse and get him ready to go," he said as he handed his sister the gallop saddle and bridle.

Kaitlin set the saddle over the stall door and gave her brother a sour look. "I can baby Ranger if I want to. He'll run better for me. You'll see."

Troy gave her a doubtful look. "He'd better run a faster time than he did when we hauled him to the track for his official work."

Kaitlin handed Ashleigh a body brush, and they worked together to groom the dust from the bay gelding's sleek coat.

"Your horse didn't run much faster," Kaitlin quipped.

Troy handed the saddle cloth to Ashleigh. She placed it on Ranger's back while Kaitlin settled the lightweight gallop saddle into place.

"The difference," Troy said, "is that the jockey was holding Dancer back while Ranger's rider was pushing him as fast as he could go."

Ashleigh saw the hurt look on Kaitlin's face. Their eyes met as she passed her cousin the bridle. "He'll do fine. Don't worry," she said encouragingly.

Kaitlin led Ranger from the barn, and Jim gave Troy a leg up.

"Backtrack this colt around the turn, then go once around slow before you work him, Troy," Jim said.

"Come on, Ash!" Kaitlin grabbed Ashleigh's arm and pulled her around the corner of the barn.

Ashleigh was a little surprised when she first caught sight of the training track. There were no rails circling the sand track, just a plowed oval path that looked to be about a half mile in length. It was no wonder she hadn't seen it the day before, when they were out riding. "Where are the rails?" she asked.

Kaitlin steered Ashleigh toward a small set of home-made wooden bleachers. "Do you know what it would cost to put a rail fence around that track?" she asked. "My parents don't have that kind of money."

Ashleigh settled onto the wooden bench. "But how do you keep the horses on the track?"

Kaitlin laughed. "Sometimes you don't. Troy's cut out through the desert several times. The older horses usually stay on the course, but the young ones can be a problem."

"Here he comes," Ashleigh said as she watched Troy

turn Ranger to face the inside rail for a moment before trotting him the correct way of the track.

Kaitlin sat forward and gripped the sides of the bench. "Come on, Ranger," she whispered. "You can do it."

Ranger broke into a leisurely canter, bobbing his head and playing with the bit as he passed.

"He looks kind of lazy today," Ashleigh observed. "What kind of time did he run last time he worked?"

Kaitlin shrugged. "It wasn't that great," she admitted. "He ran a half mile in fifty-three and change."

Ashleigh's eyes followed the gelding's slow, steady progress around the track. "Maybe he didn't feel very good that day and he'll do better this time," she said hopefully.

As the horse and rider approached the half-mile pole, Troy settled low over Ranger's withers and asked him to run. The little bay extended his stride, but he didn't seem to pick up much speed. Troy scrubbed the reins up and down the horse's neck, trying to interest Ranger in running, but the horse only flicked his black-tipped ears and continued at his rated pace.

On the final run down the stretch, Troy pulled his whip and popped the colt lightly on the haunches.

"Don't whip him!" Kaitlin cried.

Ashleigh saw Ranger's ears flatten against his head.

Then the bay gelding darted off the track and through the sagebrush. Ashleigh gasped as she watched Ranger dodge through the brush, jumping the lower bushes and bucking when he hit a clear spot.

"*Ride 'em, cowboy!*" Kaitlin hollered as she roared with laughter.

Ashleigh was stunned. Troy could be seriously hurt if he got bucked off in the brush. "Why are you laughing?" she said in confusion. "Troy and Ranger could be hurt out there." If they had been back in Kentucky at Churchill Downs and a horse tore off the track on a bucking spree, there would have been a dozen trainers and grooms and one very upset owner running after the pair, trying to prevent a tragedy.

"Troy won't get bucked off Ranger," Kaitlin said with a note of pride in her voice. "He's a great bronc rider. He even rides in the rodeos sometimes." She shared a smile with her father, who stood on the bleachers watching the horse and rider kick up dust. "Ranger has done this before," Kaitlin said. "He's a tough little horse. You don't have to worry about him getting hurt. Besides, Troy should have known better than to use the whip on him."

Ashleigh shook her head in disbelief. She was going to have a lot of stories to tell everyone when she got home. And she was definitely going to have her work cut out for her here. Kaitlin and Ranger were going to be a big challenge. She hoped she could be of help.

Troy finally got Ranger pulled up and brought him back onto the track. Ashleigh could tell by the hard set of his mouth that he wasn't pleased. He bumped the gelding into a hard run and circled the track one more time.

Jim turned to Kaitlin as the girls left their seats to catch Ranger as he came off the track after his work. "I know you think it's pretty funny that Ranger took off through the sage with your brother," he said to Kaitlin. "But your colt has got to get his mind on his business. If Ranger doesn't shape up, he's not going to do very well at the track," he warned. "This is money for your college fund, Kate. You need to get a handle on that colt."

Kaitlin bowed her head and kicked at the dirt. "Ranger doesn't like it when Troy hits him with the whip," she said in her horse's defense.

Jim scratched his chin. "It's not just today's shenanigans," he said as he nodded for the girls to take Ranger back to the barn to cool him out. "Ranger plays around almost every time he's out there. You coddle this colt too much," he said. "He won't get down to business because he's too busy being spoiled."

Ashleigh saw the I-told-you-so smile Troy gave his

sister when he dismounted and handed her the reins. Kaitlin snatched the reins from her brother's hands.

"Come on, Ash," Kaitlin said, stomping off. "They're all wrong. Ranger is going to do fine," she added with more bravado than she seemed to feel.

As Ashleigh watched the little bay gelding nibble on Kaitlin's shirt and follow her back to the barn like a puppy, she had the feeling that Troy and his father were right. Ranger was in big trouble, and Kaitlin didn't even realize it.

5

"Ashleigh, you can't wear *those* boots!" Kaitlin cried.

Ashleigh looked down at her newly polished black leather English riding boots. "Why not?" she asked in confusion.

"Because we're going to a *rodeo*," Kaitlin said, shaking her head.

Ashleigh stared at her cousin, not understanding what Kaitlin was trying to say.

Kaitlin tossed her hands up in exasperation. "A rodeo is one of the most western experiences you can get," she explained. "You can't wear *English* boots to a *western* event. We'd get laughed right out of the stands—especially if you wear them on the outside of your jeans."

Ashleigh frowned. "But they're the only boots I have."

Kaitlin opened her closet door and rummaged

through a pile of shoes and boots. "Here," she said as she produced a pair of brown leather cowboy boots with a pretty design on the toe. "We wear the same size. These should fit you."

Ashleigh took off her boots and pulled on the fancy pair of cowboy boots. She went to the mirror and turned in both directions. "I like them," she said. The heel felt a little higher than her English boots, but Kaitlin had broken them in and they felt comfortable.

"They look great on you, Ash," Kaitlin said. "Now, let me put a braid in your hair and you'll be ready to go."

Troy hollered down the hallway, "Hurry up, girls! We're leaving in five minutes."

When Kaitlin was done with Ashleigh's hair, they rushed out to join the others in the truck.

"Wait," Kaitlin said. "You're missing one thing." She grabbed a black Stetson cowboy hat from the hat rack in the hallway and placed it on Ashleigh's head. "Now you look like a real cowgirl. Let's go!"

The drive to the Reno Rodeo grounds was fascinating for Ashleigh. It had been dark when they'd driven from the airport, so she hadn't been able to see anything. Now she could see the rolling foothills that gave way to large mountains on one side and a long valley on the other.

As they got closer to town, more houses appeared on

the hillsides. Some of them were old ranch dwellings, and others were new housing projects that had sprung up next to them.

Soon they pulled onto the rodeo grounds. Ashleigh could see all the competitors' trucks and horse trailers parked in the back, where the barns were. The Gilberts parked in the front of the lot with the rest of the spectators.

Ashleigh couldn't help but smile as they joined the people filing toward the admission gate. She'd never seen so many jeans, Stetson hats, and cowboy boots in her life. There was a buzz of excitement in the air, and she was happy to be a part of it.

Once they got inside and found their seats, Kaitlin wanted to go look at the bucking stock. "Come on, Ash," she said as they made their way down the steps of the grandstands. "You've never seen a real bucking horse up close."

Several cowboys tipped their hats to them as they passed. Ashleigh was amazed at how young some of them looked. The older cowboys were tall and lean, with lined faces that showed years of hard work.

"Here we are," Kaitlin said as she stopped in front of a large five-board pen that held at least thirty horses.

Ashleigh peeked through the boards. *They aren't a very pretty lot,* she thought as she took in the thick-boned, Roman-nosed horses that stood near her, staring back with curious eyes. Her father called those types of horses "hammerheads," and it was generally known that they could be very stubborn. There were a few decent-looking horses in the bunch, and lots of pintos, buckskins, and duns. Ashleigh noticed that most of the bucking stock were small, stout horses with a lot of muscle.

A buckskin horse with a long black mane and tail pushed through the herd, nipping at the flanks of any others that got in his way. He was a little taller than the rest, with a thick neck and well-muscled haunches. "Wow, look at that one!" Ashleigh said. "He looks like he could really buck."

"You've got a good eye, Ash," Kaitlin said. "That's ol' Cyclone. He's one of the best bucking horses in the country right now."

"Will we get to see him tonight?" Ashleigh asked.

"Oh, yes." Kaitlin laughed. "Half the crowd is here to watch this horse, and all the cowboys are hoping they draw him for the bucking events. If they can stay on his back for the full eight seconds, he'll give them such a good ride that they're almost guaranteed to win," she explained. "But there aren't very many cowboys who have made it the full eight seconds on Cyclone's back. He's on his way to becoming a rodeo legend."

"Wow, I can't wait to see that!" Ashleigh said.

Kaitlin pulled Ashleigh away from the pen. "We'd better get back. Shelby is riding in the opening ceremonies."

They got to their seats just as the national anthem began to play. Everyone stood facing the center of the arena. As the first words of the song began, a horse and rider burst through the far gate, racing around the arena with the American flag. The girl on the beautiful palomino was dressed in red, white, and blue and had the same honey-colored hair as the horse she rode. It was Shelby Jeffrey.

Shelby made a round of the arena and then brought her horse to a sliding stop in the center of the ring for the remainder of the tune. When the anthem was over, a great cheer went up, and Shelby made another speedy lap around the arena before exiting through the gate at a dead run.

Ashleigh felt a pang of jealousy over Shelby's riding skills. She had to admit the girl had ability. "Why do they race around so fast?" she asked as she watched the other girls who carried flags with advertisers' names on them racing around the ring in the same manner.

Kaitlin shrugged. "It's tradition. I think it just shows their skill at handling a fast-moving horse. I think it would be a lot of fun," she admitted. "My parents said I can try out for the flag team in a couple of years."

"That would be pretty cool," Ashleigh said as she

took her seat and reached for her camera. The first event was about to start. "What's the wild-horse race?" she asked as she looked at her rodeo program.

Kaitlin sat forward in her seat. "You're going to love this one. It's pretty funny."

Several teams, each of them made up of four men, stepped into the arena.

"See the big guys standing next to the bucking chutes?" Kaitlin said. "There's a wild horse wearing a halter with a long rope behind each of those gates. The goal is for that big guy to hold the horse still long enough for his partners to get a saddle on it. Then one of the cowboys will get up on the horse and try to ride it across the finish line," she explained as she pointed to the two barrels at the other end of the arena. "The first one across is the winner."

A starting gun blasted, and all the gates swung outward. Moments later the entire arena was in total chaos as the unbroken horses attempted to break free of their handlers while the cowboys tried to saddle them and hop aboard. Ashleigh and her cousins roared with laughter as some of the men were dragged across the dirt, looking as if they were skiing behind a boat, while others watched their saddles being thrown high into the air by an uncooperative bronc. One of the teams had gotten their horse saddled and the rider was hanging on for dear life, trying to stay in the saddle until his horse ran across the finish line, bucking the entire time.

Ashleigh snapped several pictures as the cowboys and their wild mounts came close to the grandstands. After several long moments, while the wild ones ran to and fro, a small cowboy on a fat bay mare made it across the line and was declared the winner. The other competitors gave up their attempts and gave one another a clap on the back as they walked from the arena.

"Have you ever seen anything like that?" Troy asked.

Ashleigh smiled. "It kind of reminds me of the first class of the show season," she joked.

Everyone laughed, and Kaitlin slapped her a high five. They settled into their seats and waited for the bareback bronc contest to start. In between each event, a rodeo princess or flag girl entered the ring carrying a flag with an advertiser's name on it and raced around the arena at top speed. A couple of the horses spooked at people in the grandstands, but the skillful riders stayed in their saddles.

The rodeo announcer called the first horse and rider, and chute number one popped open. The bucking bronco charged from the chute, running several steps before he broke in two and bucked as hard as he could. The cowboy stayed on the bronco's back for the full eight seconds, qualifying him for the ride.

The next two riders didn't fare as well. One fell off

the first jump out of the gate, and the other cowboy got bucked high into the air only seconds into the ride.

"Cyclone is next," Jim said.

Linda reminded Ashleigh to get her camera ready. "This horse has bucked off his last twenty-five riders," she said. "But tonight Shay Mendoza drew him. Shay is the top cowboy in the country right now. Cyclone may have met his match."

The announcer listed both the cowboy's and horse's recent accomplishments. Then the gate swung open, and Cyclone burst into the arena, jumping high into the air and coming down stiff-legged before taking flight again and swapping ends.

Ashleigh couldn't believe the punishment the cowboy was taking as his body snapped around with all the sudden direction changes. As the pair neared the eight-second mark, the audience began to go wild. A great roar filled the air as the audience prepared to witness the cowboy's triumph over the famous bronc. Then a sudden spin of the crafty buckskin's powerful body sent the cowboy careening off the left side of the horse. He hit the dirt and rolled at the same moment the eight-second bell rang.

At first the crowd voiced a loud, disappointed "Ohhh." Then the bronc circled the ring in triumph with his tail over his back and his proud head held high, and the people in the grandstands went wild.

They stood and cheered for the buckskin horse, which made two more laps of the ring, managing to avoid the outriders, before he voluntarily went through the gate to join his buddies in the pen.

Ashleigh watched many more events. The bulldogging boggled her mind. Why any rider would want to jump off a perfectly good horse onto the horns of a running steer and wrestle it to the ground was beyond her. She watched the roping events with interest, trying to see how they did it. After witnessing the skill of the ropers, she felt even worse about having challenged Shelby to the contest.

When the bull riding came, Ashleigh pulled out her camera and got several great shots of the brave cowboys riding the large Brahma bulls. She was surprised at the skill and bravery of the rodeo clowns, who taunted the bulls when a rider was thrown so that the cowboy could make a safe escape.

Ashleigh laughed when a clown with knee-length shorts and bright purple suspenders ran from an angry bull and jumped into a special barrel. The bull charged the barrel, smacking it hard and sending it several feet into the air. The crowd gasped until the barrel rolled to a stop and the clown popped out with a big bouquet of daisies, which he presented to a girl in the nearby grandstand. Everyone clapped and sat back in their seats.

Kaitlin opened her program. "The only thing left is the barrel racing," she said. "This is the only event in the rodeo that women compete in."

"Why is that?" Ashleigh said curiously. She thought about all the women who had broken into owning, training, and jockeying at the racetrack. What was so different about the rodeo?

Kaitlin shrugged. "Tradition, I guess."

Troy laughed as he leaned over to whisper in Ashleigh's ear. "The truth is, it's a very rough sport, and women have too much common sense to climb on those wild horses and bulls for no good reason other than a couple of broken ribs."

Ashleigh laughed along with her cousin. One thing was for sure—nobody would ever catch her on the back of one of those crazy bulls, which weighed almost as much as a small car and liked to eat cowboys for lunch.

They watched several young women run the barrels for a time. They were all pretty close, but one of the girls tipped a barrel over as she went around it, and so she got time added onto her score as a penalty.

"Why do some of the riders take the left barrel first, others the right?" Ashleigh asked.

"It depends on whether your horse turns best to the right or left," Linda said. "If you circle to the right first, then you have to make two left-hand turns on your next two barrels. If you go the left first, then you run the opposite."

"Which way does Flash go?" Ashleigh asked just as Shelby stepped through the gate on her palomino.

"Flash runs one right and two left, just like most horses do," Kaitlin said. "Watch and see how Shelby does it."

As Ashleigh watched, the skilled cowgirl raced around the barrels at top speed and crossed the finish line just a fifth of a second behind the second-place girl. The event looked like a lot of fun, but she wondered how she was ever going to beat Shelby Jeffrey, cowgirl extraordinaire.

6

"I'm never going to get this right!" Ashleigh cried to Troy and Kaitlin as the rope she was twirling came crashing down on her head before she'd even had a chance to toss it. "I just can't do it!"

"Here, let me show you again," Troy said as he coiled the rope once more and then twirled it over his head. "You've got to keep the rhythm going so your loop doesn't collapse," he instructed. "Then, when you're ready, you just toss the loop toward your target and let go. See?" he said in satisfaction as the perfect loop settled over the horns of the fake steer ten feet away.

"No, I *don't* see," Ashleigh replied angrily as she folded her arms across her chest and debated going into the house to read one of her horse magazines. She was *never* going to get the hang of roping.

"Come on, Ash," Troy cajoled as he handed her the rope again. "You picked up barrel racing like you were born to it. You even did well your first time at pole bending. Don't give up on roping just because it's a little more difficult."

Ashleigh stared at the back door of the house and then at Kaitlin's pleading look. She snatched the rope from Troy's hands. "Oh, all right. I'll give it one more try." She made a big loop in her rope, just as Troy had taught her, and then with a quick flick of her wrist sent it into the air over her head. She used the circling motion of her wrist to keep the rope in the air, speeding up when she sensed that the loop was ready to collapse.

"You're doing it, Ash!" Kaitlin said excitedly. "Quick, toss it over the steer's horns before you lose it!"

Ashleigh let loose the spinning rope and watched it sail through the air, but it landed at least five feet from her target. Everyone stood in silence for a moment. Then Ashleigh's head jerked around at the sound of clapping coming from the edge of the property.

Shelby!

The blond cowgirl sat astride her golden horse not fifty feet away. Ashleigh frowned heavily as she wondered how long the girl had been there.

"Nice toss," Shelby said.

Troy gathered the rope and coiled it back up, hanging it over the horns of the steer. "Give her a break, Shelby. I remember your first time trying to rope. You were just as bad."

Ashleigh knew that her cousin was trying to stick up for her, but saying that she was bad only made her feel worse. She gave the blond girl a glare, then crammed her hands into her pockets and stomped toward the house.

I should cancel this stupid contest, Ashleigh thought as she opened the back door and entered the warm interior of the house. She had more important things to work on. Getting Ranger to the racetrack was a lot more important than beating Shelby. But besting the rodeo queen at her own game would definitely be fun, Ashleigh decided. Maybe she'd give the gymkhana lessons a little more time and see if she got any better before making a final decision.

Ashleigh spent the next several days trying to improve her new skills. She was making progress with the roping, but she was having a very difficult time of it. Barrel racing and pole bending were her favorites. Flash was a very athletic mare, and Ashleigh got along well with her.

As she hosed the black-and-white paint down after a hard workout, her mind wandered to Edgardale. She wasn't sure what had set it off, but she was having a persistent bout of homesickness that day. Flash nuzzled her arm, and she felt her heart constrict in her chest. What was Stardust doing at that moment? Had any more foals been born? She sighed heavily as she realized she even missed Caroline. It would be another five weeks before she went home. She wondered if she would last that long. This vacation had been a lot of fun so far, but she hadn't counted on being so homesick.

"Ashleigh," Linda called from the house, "there's a phone call for you."

Kaitlin took the lead rope from Ashleigh's hands. "I'll put Flash away. You go take your call. Tell my mom I'll be up after I check on Ranger," she said. "Tomorrow's his big race. I want to make sure everything is perfect."

Ashleigh sprinted toward the house. Linda handed her the phone and indicated that she could sit in the chair in the corner.

"Ash, it's me, Mona," the voice came over the line.

"Mona!" Ashleigh cried happily. "I was just thinking about home."

"I wanted to call and see how you were doing," Mona said. "Are you having a good time?"

Ashleigh felt her spirits lift immediately. She told Mona all about her stay, including the challenge Shelby Jeffrey had laid down and the new horse events she was learning. She listened closely while Mona filled her in on all the happenings around home and how the local show season was progressing.

"I've been riding Stardust for you," Mona said. "But she doesn't seem to be losing any weight. Maybe your parents need to keep her off the pasture for a while. The grass is pretty rich this year."

"I'll talk to my parents about it," Ashleigh said. "We're going to race Kaitlin's and Troy's geldings tomorrow. I'll call home when we get back from the racetrack."

She said goodbye to Mona and hung up the phone, feeling much better than she had a few moments before. The next day she would get to talk to her family. Her heart felt lighter already. Ashleigh whistled a tune as she stepped out the back door to go help her cousin ready her horse for the upcoming race.

"Wow, you weren't kidding when you said this was a small track," Ashleigh said as she viewed the four lines of portable stalls and the few standing barns, which looked as though they were ready for the woodpile.

The Gilberts' truck and trailer bumped down the dirt road between the barns and came to a halt in front of the sign that marked the cluster of stalls as the receiving barn.

Ashleigh got out and stretched her legs. "Is that the racetrack?" she asked in surprise as she viewed the small oval with sharp turns. As she looked across the track to the small wooden grandstand, a tractor went by, pulling the starting gate. The starting gate had chicken wire on the front doors. Ashleigh was shocked. She wasn't sure whether to laugh at the absurdity or be concerned for the horses and riders.

As she took in the chipped white paint on the inner and outer rails of the track, a slow smile spread over her face. She wondered what her trainer friend Mike Smith would have to say about running one of his stakes horses at this bush track. One thing was for sure—this was a far cry from Churchill Downs!

"Ashleigh, can you put Ranger's and Dancer's buckets in their stalls?" Jim called as he backed the geldings from the horse trailer.

Ashleigh hung the buckets and reached for the hose to give the horses water. Ranger was turned into the stall next to his stablemate. The little bay made several rounds of the stall, lowering his head to sniff the straw bedding, then came to the door and called to the horses across the way.

"We've got a couple of hours before the race," Kaitlin said as she ran her hand down Ranger's neck to help calm him. "Let's give him a good brushing, then let him settle down while we go watch the first couple of races from the front side." She gave Ranger a kiss on the nose. "You're entered in the same race as Dancer today. You're going to beat him by a mile, aren't you, boy?"

Ashleigh laughed. "That's going to be quite a feat, considering they're only running three-quarters of a mile."

Together they brushed Ranger until his coat gleamed. After hanging his racing bridle outside the stall, they walked to the front side to watch the horses going over for the first race.

"Boy, this sure is different from Churchill Downs or Keeneland," Ashleigh said as she watched the trainers circle their horses around a small walking ring filled with pine chips. There wasn't even a real jockey's quarters, she noted. There was only a portable trailer, which the men and women jockeys had to share.

Kaitlin found a spot along the short cyclone fence that bordered the walking ring, and made room for Ashleigh. "Yes, it's really different, but different can be fun."

Ashleigh peeked at the racing program the man next to her was carrying. The first race was a maiden quarter horse race for three-year-olds going 220 yards. She was shocked to see that the purse was only twelve hundred dollars. "How can an owner or trainer make any money on that low of a purse?" she asked.

Kaitlin shrugged. "You have to win a lot of races. That's why you'll see trainers at these small tracks running their horses once every week or two."

"But won't racing that often break them down?"

The jockeys came from their quarters and were legged up onto the young quarter horses.

"Some of the horses break down, and some of them do just fine," Kaitlin said. "That part's not much different from the big tracks. Several horses have broken down in the Kentucky Derby over the last couple of years, haven't they?" she said.

A young man stepped onto the track and raised his horn to play the call to the post. Ashleigh and Kaitlin crowded in on the rail and watched the horses parade for the crowd. The odds on the tote board changed every couple of minutes.

Ashleigh pointed to the number four horse, a short, muscular chestnut with a white blaze. "It looks like he's the favorite."

Kaitlin nodded. "Yes, but the problem with these short races is that any little mishap can cost a horse the race. If number four gets bumped out of the gate, he could end up running last. Have you ever seen a race this short?" she asked.

Ashleigh shook her head.

"You're in for a real treat, Ash," Kaitlin said. "The horses start down there at the top of the chute, and they run straight down the track. The track is so short that the finish line is right before the turn."

"Isn't that a little dangerous?" Ashleigh asked as she watched the horses being loaded into the starting gate.

"I've seen a few of them bounce off the outside fence," Kaitlin said. "They cross the finish line at full speed and go immediately into the turn. Some of the horses don't switch into the correct lead. That makes it very difficult to make the turn."

"The horses have been loaded into the gate," the announcer called. "And they're off!"

Ashleigh stood on her toes to see the start. There was lots of banging around as the horses came out of the gate. She saw the number four horse stumble slightly before his rider straightened him out and asked him to run. Before she even had a chance to yell her encouragement, the field of horses raced past them in a cloud of flying dirt and churning hooves. The powerful chestnut was at the rear of the herd as the horses went around the turn eight abreast. Ashleigh was surprised that none of them hit the outside fence.

"Jeez!" Ashleigh said. "Do the Thoroughbreds run the same way? Will Ranger and Dancer be safe?"

Kaitlin shook her head. "The Thoroughbreds run longer races, so they're moving slower and they're spaced better. It's not so different from Kentucky. The track is just a lot smaller." She motioned for Ashleigh to follow her back to the walking ring. "We can watch one more race, and then we've got to head back to get Ranger ready. Troy and my dad will be taking care of Dancer."

When the next race was finished, they made their way back to the receiving barn to put the finishing touches on Ranger. Ashleigh braided a small blue pompom into his mane while Linda bridled the nervous colt. Kaitlin listened for the call to take the horses to the front side. When it finally came, Troy walked his own horse over, and Ranger was turned over to Jim while the girls ran on ahead to get a good spot on the rail.

"Did you bring your camera, Ash?" Kaitlin asked. "I want to get some pictures of Ranger in his first race. He looks so good in his racing saddle and number cloth."

The jockeys mounted up, and the horses stepped onto the track. Ashleigh snapped several photos of Dancer and Ranger as they passed, but she wasn't sure how the photos of Ranger were going to turn out. The gelding constantly moved his head and played with his bit. When they trotted off to the starting gate, the pony horse rider practically had to drag Ranger to the gate. The horse seemed to be more interested in playing than racing.

"This is a six-furlong race, and the track is a half mile long, so they'll start at the opposite side of the track and pass us twice," Linda said as everyone took their places on the fence. "At least there are no trees in the center of the track to block our view."

Ashleigh was surprised to see Ranger load right in after he'd been fussing during the entire post parade. Dancer paused for a moment before loading in next to Ranger.

Kaitlin covered her eyes. "I can't watch this, Ash," she cried. "It's too nerve-wracking."

But when the announcer hollered, "They're off!" Kaitlin immediately opened her eyes. "Where is he?"

Troy pointed to the back of the herd. "He had his head down when the gate popped. He got out last. But look at Dancer!" he said excitedly. "My horse is running second!"

"Come on, Ranger!" Kaitlin hollered as she banged on the rail. "Catch up to your stablemate. I know you can do it!"

But Ranger stayed where he was, galloping along behind the rest of the horses. Dancer moved up along the inside rail, making a bid for first place. Ashleigh didn't know what to do. She wanted to cheer for Dancer, but Ranger was running dead last, and she didn't want to upset Kaitlin.

The announcer's voice boomed over the speaker

system. "Dancer's Pride moves up to take the lead as they come out of the turn and down the stretch. My Honey drops back to second, Fast Charger is third, and Bold Ranger is in last place."

"You can do it, Ranger! I know you can!" Kaitlin cried. But the enthusiasm in her voice faded as Ranger remained in the rear, galloping along as though he were out for a Sunday ride.

"Dancer's Pride wins by three lengths!" the announcer called, and a cheer went up from the crowd.

Troy pumped his fist in victory and hugged his parents. Ashleigh smiled and shook his hand, then turned her attention back to Kaitlin as Ranger galloped across the finish line many lengths behind the next horse. The roar of the crowd was deafening, but Ashleigh could hear her cousin's heart breaking from where she stood.

7

Kaitlin bowed her head and stood silent for a moment, then lifted her chin and wiped away a tear. "There must have been something wrong," she said.

Troy smirked. "Yeah, your horse can't run," he teased, watching as Dancer's jockey trotted him back to the winner's circle.

"Troy!" Jim said sharply as he gave his son a disapproving stare. "That wasn't a very nice thing to say to your sister."

Troy hung his head, having the good grace to be ashamed of himself. "I'm sorry, Kate. Ranger probably just didn't feel well today," he apologized. "I'll help you with him when we get back home. Maybe he'll win his next race."

Kaitlin nodded her acceptance of his apology and waited for Ranger to return. While the rest of the family posed in the winner's circle, she took Ranger's reins and waited for the jockey to pull his saddle from the gelding's back.

"You can get in the win photo, Ash," Kaitlin said as she eyed the gaiety in the winner's circle with longing. "It's okay."

Ashleigh shook her head. "I'll go back to the barn with you," she said. "You'll need help bathing Ranger."

They walked in silence for several moments, then Kaitlin spoke up. "I really didn't expect Ranger to win his first time out," she said quietly. "But I thought he'd at least run in the middle of the pack." She put her hand on the gelding's neck as they exited the track into the stable area. "How could you let me down like that, boy?"

Ashleigh ran ahead to the stall and filled the wash bucket with warm water. They had no wash rack at the receiving barn, so they'd have to give Ranger his bath out of a bucket. When they were finished, Kaitlin walked the colt to cool him off while they waited for the others to return.

"Could you take the wash bucket and Dancer's halter to the test barn, Ash?" Kaitlin asked as she stopped to give Ranger a small drink of water before continuing with the walk. "Since Dancer won, they'll have to cool him out in the test barn so they can test him for drugs."

Ashleigh gathered the things. "I wouldn't think they

would bother spending the money to test the horses at this small a track," she said in surprise. "The purses are so tiny."

Kaitlin stopped to give Ranger a bigger drink of water. She put her hand to his chest to see if he was cooling out properly. "It doesn't matter how small the purse is, Ash. People are still serious about winning, and some people are very unscrupulous. They'll do anything to win."

"There's your family with Dancer," Ashleigh said, pointing to where they were stepping off the track. "I'll take this stuff to them and be right back."

Linda met Ashleigh at the gate of the testing barn. Only licensed owners, trainers, and grooms were allowed inside. "How's Kaitlin taking this?" she asked.

Ashleigh handed the bucket and halter to Kaitlin's mom. She crammed her hands into her pockets as she thought about how to answer the question. "I think she's just really sad," Ashleigh said finally. "Kaitlin thought Ranger would run a little better than he did."

Linda nodded. "That colt doesn't seem to have his mind on racing. And Kaitlin probably *does* spoil him a little too much," she said with a smile. "Thanks for bringing Dancer's things, Ash. We'll be ready to leave as soon as he's cooled out and tested. Tell Kaitlin to get everything packed into the truck when she's done with Ranger."

A half hour later the horses were loaded, and they pulled onto the road heading for home. For a while everyone sat in silence, not sure what to say. Ashleigh could tell that Troy wanted to celebrate, and rightfully so. His horse had won on his very first outing. But Kaitlin looked as though she wanted to cry. Finally their father broke the silence.

"Look, folks, we've had a tough day. One of our horses did very well, and the other had a rough time. Let's just be happy that Dancer won, and we'll try a little harder with Ranger, okay?"

Kaitlin sat still for several moments, staring at the Ponderosa pines and redwoods that lined the northern California highway. Finally she leaned forward and mussed her brother's hair. "I'm sorry I'm being such a spoilsport. Congratulations on winning with Dancer."

Troy grinned as he smoothed his hair back into place. "Thanks, Kate. Ranger's time will come. We've just got to work a little harder with him."

The rest of the trip home was made in companionable silence as everyone listened to the crooners belting out country songs on the local radio station.

When they pulled into the Gilberts' ranch, Ashleigh helped unload the horses, then asked for permission to call her parents. It was almost six o'clock in Nevada. It would be nine o'clock at home. Everyone would be getting ready for bed.

Ashleigh dialed the number and counted the rings. After the third chime, she heard her mother's voice on the other end of the line.

"Hi, Mom," Ashleigh said, glad to hear the sound of her mother's voice. She didn't know whether to ask first about the family or about the horses, so she just let her mother begin with what had been happening on the farm. She spoke to everyone in the family, finding out what had happened in her absence and telling them about her vacation in Nevada and all of the fun things they had done so far.

"How's Stardust doing?" she asked her father when it was his turn to talk.

Mr. Griffen made a tsking sound. "We've been cutting Stardust's feed back, and Mona has been riding her, but she doesn't seem to be losing much weight. Maybe it'll all come off at once," he said. "With some luck we'll have her back in shape by the time you get home."

"What do you think it could be?" Ashleigh asked, wondering why nothing they did seemed to be helping. "I talked to Mona yesterday, and she said the pasture grass was really rich this year. Do you think taking Stardust off the pasture for a while will help?"

"That's my next step," Mr. Griffen said. "Don't worry, Ash," he assured her. "We'll get Stardust squared away. She's in good hands."

Ashleigh nodded. She knew her father was a great horseman. He and her mother would figure out the problem before she got home. She changed the subject and continued the conversation. When she was all talked out, Ashleigh hung up the phone. She had thought she would feel a little brighter, but her homesickness was worse than ever. Her cousins entered the house a few minutes later and asked about her family. Ashleigh filled them in on the details while Linda pulled a frozen pizza out of the refrigerator.

"It's been a long day today," Linda said. "Dinner will be pizza and salad. We can eat in the living room on TV trays and watch a video. Then it'll be time for bed."

Ashleigh helped Kaitlin make the salad, then they set up the TV trays in the living room and picked out a video. It was a western about a pioneer family that moved out west to start a cattle ranch. It was sad in places and made Ashleigh miss her family even more.

That night Ashleigh lay in bed staring at the ceiling. She felt tears burning the backs of her eyes. She knew she shouldn't feel this way. Her cousins had been great, and she'd had a fun time so far. But she still missed her family and her horses.

Kaitlin stirred next to her, and Ashleigh thought she heard her cousin sniff. She lay very still and listened. It came again, and this time there was no doubt about it. Kaitlin was crying.

"Are you all right?" Ashleigh asked. "What's the matter, Kaitlin?"

Kaitlin remained silent.

Ashleigh put aside her own sadness as she worried about her cousin. "Is there anything I can do?" she asked.

Kaitlin sniffed again. "Not unless you can give Ranger wings," she said, and hiccuped as she tried to laugh.

Ashleigh turned on her side and tucked her hand under the pillow. "Not every horse can win its first race, the way Dancer did," she said. "Ranger will do better his next time out. He acted like he didn't really know what he was doing out there," Ashleigh went on. "Maybe next time he'll figure it out."

Kaitlin hiccuped again, and then burst into a fit of giggles.

"What's so funny?" Ashleigh asked.

Kaitlin sat up in bed and punched her pillow. "*Us*," she said. "You're lying there feeling homesick, and I'm lying here being horse-sick. We're a real sorry pair."

Ashleigh nodded in agreement. "What can we do about it?"

Kaitlin drew her knees close so she could rest her chin on them. "There's one cure I know that works every time."

"What's that?" Ashleigh asked curiously.

"Tomorrow we're going to go mustang scouting," Kaitlin said.

"Really?" Ashleigh replied.

Kaitlin nodded in the darkness. "Yep. Once you see that wild herd running on the range with their manes and tails flying in the wind, all your cares just seem to slip away."

"Do you know where to find them?" Ashleigh asked excitedly.

Kaitlin settled back under the covers. "They usually graze in the next valley over," she said. "It's about an hour's ride, but it's worth it. Go to sleep, Ash. We'll get started early tomorrow."

Ashleigh closed her eyes and tried to picture the sight of wild mustangs on the land. Since it was June, there would most likely be foals on the ground, too. She pulled up the covers and smiled to herself. She was feeling better already.

The rooster crowed at dawn, but this time Ashleigh didn't mind. She was ready to get up and get saddled. Somewhere over the hill there were bands of wild mustangs waiting!

Kaitlin sat up in bed and stretched. "I'll run out and feed the horses real quick while you pour the breakfast cereal and pack us some sandwiches and a couple of apples. We'll be gone for a few hours."

They quickly changed, and each went about her job. By the time the rest of the family was just getting out of bed, they were on the trail heading for the nearby mountain range. Since they were going to be traveling a lot of miles, Ashleigh decided to ride the Arabian mare, Ariel, and Kaitlin rode her mother's horse, Koda.

It didn't take Ashleigh long to figure out what Kaitlin had meant about the gray Arabian being a handful. The mare was quicker than a cat and didn't hesitate to jump and snort at anything that moved along the trail. Ashleigh knew that when she was riding this horse she'd never be able to let her guard down.

But one thing was for sure—Ariel could go forever. They had left the barn at a trot. When they reached the foothills, the little gray mare charged up the path, eager to get to the top, but Kaitlin's horse was badly winded. They decided to walk the horses up the inclines and carefully trot down the easy slopes.

After an hour of up-and-down travel, they came to a place that looked out over a small valley.

"It'll take twenty minutes to ride to the valley floor," Kaitlin said. "There's a spring down by that copse of junipers, and the mustangs like to gather there in the morning."

They rode carefully down the hillside, coming to the edge of a grassy field.

"Wow, you don't see much grass around here," Ashleigh said as she let Ariel drop her head to crop. The mare had worked hard. She deserved a treat.

Kaitlin pointed to the small stream that ran through the meadow. "This part of the valley has a few springs that keep things watered," she explained. "In really dry years, even the springs dry up. Then the mustangs come down into the residential areas to look for water. A few of them of them have been hit by cars. It's really sad."

Ashleigh ran her fingers through the Arabian's mane. "How did the mustangs get here?"

"Several hundred years ago the Spanish explorers brought their Andalusian and Barb horses with them when they first started exploring North America," Kaitlin explained. "Some of the horses escaped, and some of them were set free when the explorers returned to their homeland. The horses bred and formed huge herds that used to roam the land."

Ashleigh shaded her eyes from the sun as she searched the hillsides and meadows for wild horses. "Wouldn't that have been something to see?" she said.

Kaitlin nodded. "Eventually the Indians rounded up the best of the wild ones to use for hunting bison, and the cowboys gathered what they could for use in herding cattle. As the settlers moved west they turned out their own stock to breed with the mustangs, so most of the horses you see today aren't a true representation of the original mustangs."

"I've seen pictures of them in books," Ashleigh said. "But I never dreamed I'd see a wild mustang in person. Where do you suppose they're hiding?"

Kaitlin gave a gentle tug on the reins, lifting Koda's head. "We'll have to go looking for them," she said. "This valley makes a bend around the mountain. Let's ride in that direction."

Ashleigh followed her cousin down a well-worn path. "Is this the trail the mustangs follow?"

Kaitlin turned in the saddle and held her finger to her lips. "We don't want to scare the mustangs off," she whispered. "The mustangs follow all of these trails." She pointed to a large mound of horse manure. "See that?"

Ashleigh's brows drew together. "Who would haul a load of manure way out here to dump it?" she asked in confusion.

Kaitlin stopped her mare so that Ashleigh could pull her horse alongside. "That's a stallion mound," she quietly explained. "That's how they mark their territory. It tells the other stallions to keep away."

Ashleigh was amazed. She'd never seen anything

like that before. She was about to ask another question when a flock of bluish birds rose from the sagebrush at the side of the trail, making an awful racket and scaring her horse. Ashleigh grabbed a handful of mane, righting herself in the saddle as she pulled on the reins to stop the mare from bolting. "What was that?" she cried as she tried to calm her horse.

Kaitlin quieted her own mare. "Those are what we call scrub jays. When you startle them, they take to the air, making a horrible racket. It kind of sounds like they're laughing, doesn't it? I hope we don't run into any more of them," she said. "They'll scare off the mustangs."

They rounded a bend in the trail, and Ashleigh halted her horse, staring across the valley. "Is that them?" she asked excitedly, pointing to a band of horses grazing across the way.

There were at least twelve horses in the herd. Most of them were adults, but Ashleigh could see several yearlings and a couple of foals, too. Most of the horses were bays and sorrels, but there was one red roan and an older gray mare. Ashleigh noticed that they seemed to have good weight, and their coats were sleek and shiny. She guessed that the small herd must spend most of their time grazing on this rare, lush field of grass.

Kaitlin pulled her horse to a stop and smiled. "Aren't they awesome?" she whispered.

"Can we get any closer?" Ashleigh asked. "It looks like there are some foals in the herd. I'd really like to see them up close."

Kaitlin started her mare forward. "I ride out here a lot, and they're used to seeing me, but we probably won't get very close. The stallion won't let us."

They rode straight toward the herd. As they got nearer Ashleigh could see the small, sturdy build of the horses. None of them seemed to be over fifteen hands high. Their intelligent eyes and little fox ears turned in their direction, watching curiously as they approached. When they were within two hundred yards of the herd, a golden palomino came charging down the mountainside with its head raised high as it snorted a warning.

"Is that the stallion?" Ashleigh said in awe. The palomino lifted its tail over its back and took off in a high-stepping prance, trotting back and forth in front of the herd as it snorted nervously.

Kaitlin pointed to a short, stout black horse that came racing down the hillside, neighing a challenge as his long, tangled mane floated in the wind. "*That's* the stallion," she said in admiration. "The palomino is the lead mare."

Ashleigh watched, holding her breath, as the palomino whirled and raced away. The other horses in the herd followed, with the stallion nipping the flanks of any mares that weren't fleeing fast enough. Ashleigh was surprised at the speed of the two foals in the herd. They kept up with their mothers as they pounded across the meadow and cut up a trail on the side of the mountain. After several minutes the mustangs disappeared over the ridge, and Kaitlin and Ashleigh were left in the silence of the still meadow.

Ashleigh sat unmoving in her saddle, afraid to blink for fear the magic of the moment would be ruined. Her heart pounded, and goose bumps raced up and down her arms. In that heartbeat, with the image of the beautiful mustang herd in her mind, she knew that no matter how homesick she was or how many things went wrong, everything was worth this one special moment. It was something she would treasure for the rest of her life.

8

"The gymkhana show is this Saturday," Kaitlin said. "Do you want to try a few events?"

"What?" Ashleigh gulped. In her head she had known the show would take place this weekend, but in her heart it seemed much too early. "It's t-too soon," she sputtered. "I'm not good enough yet."

Kaitlin plopped a small barrel-racing saddle on the fence next to Ashleigh's horse. "You don't need to go out there to win the first time. Just go have fun with it and try out the course. Everybody does it."

Ashleigh shook her head adamantly. "No way!" she protested. "It's too soon. I'd look goofy out there, and Shelby would be the first one to point it out."

"You've got to quit worrying about Shelby," Kaitlin said as she ran the rubber currycomb over Tony's coat. The old buckskin sighed and cocked his back leg as he relaxed and enjoyed the rub.

"What's this for?" Ashleigh asked, pointing to the saddle that sat on the top rail of the fence.

Kaitlin grinned. "Remember how I said that you couldn't go to the rodeo in your English boots? Well, you can't go to a gymkhana riding an English saddle. It's okay for the trails, but from now on, when you're running barrels and roping, you need to use the western saddle."

Ashleigh frowned as she dragged the saddle off the fence and heaved it onto the mare's back. It was a lot heavier and bulkier than her English saddle. But her cousin had a point. She didn't want to be the only one at the gymkhana in an English saddle.

They finished saddling the horses and mounted up, going to the large arena at the back of the property. Ashleigh felt funny sitting in the western saddle. The stirrups were much bigger than her English stirrups, and they felt foreign to her feet. There was so much leather between her and her horse that she couldn't feel her horse's movements as well.

Riding in her English saddle was almost like riding bareback with stirrups. This western saddle felt strange, with its high cantle in the back and the big pommel in the front. It was going to take a lot of getting used to.

"We'll start with a couple of easy runs on the barrels," Kaitlin said. "You know how to do this pretty well, so there's no sense in wearing out your horse.

When we're done with that, you're going to try throwing a rope from the back of your horse today."

Ashleigh frowned. "I can barely rope my target when I'm standing on the ground," she grouched. "How do you expect me to do it in the saddle?" *Especially when I'm having trouble getting used to the western saddle,* she thought.

Ashleigh leaned down to pat her mare's neck. "Ouch!" she cried as the western saddle's horn gouged into her ribs.

"Oh, come on, Ash," Kaitlin said, laughing. "Quit bellyaching and give it a try. When we're done with that, I'm going to teach you a new event."

Ashleigh perked up. "As long as it doesn't have anything to do with a rope," she said.

Kaitlin pointed to a configuration of three poles, a jump, and three barrels. "You're going to weave through those poles, go over the jump, weave through the barrels, and back over the jump again."

"That sounds like fun!" Ashleigh said. "Sometimes I jump Stardust at home." She sat back in the saddle, surprised to discover that her horse's name didn't send her into a bout of homesickness anymore. It wasn't that she had quit missing her horse. But ever since seeing the wild herd of mustangs, she had decided that it was time to really enjoy her vacation.

Ashleigh bit her lip as she eyed the rope that was looped over the corner fence post. She supposed it was probably time to stop worrying so much about Shelby Jeffrey, too. She needed to spend more time trying to figure out how to help Ranger do better in his next race.

"I've got an idea," Ashleigh said, waiting until she had Kaitlin's full attention. "We'll practice all of the events, and I'll even try roping once more. But as soon as we're done, let's sit down and figure a new plan for Ranger."

"Deal!" Kaitlin said with a snappy salute as she moved to a corner of the arena so she could watch Ashleigh run the barrels. "Your technique is getting much better," she complimented Ashleigh after her first run. "Just watch that Flash doesn't start dropping her shoulder as she goes into the pocket to make the turn."

When she was done with the barrels, Ashleigh rode over to the fence to pick up her rope. She was feeling more comfortable with the saddle. Now, if only she could feel better about roping!

Kaitlin rode Tony up to the practice steer and tossed her rope, sending the loop over the horns. "Okay, now it's your turn."

Ashleigh tossed her loop several times, missing on every try.

"You're not concentrating," Kaitlin accused. "Try to remember all of the pointers that Troy gave you the other day."

Troy climbed the fence and sat on the top rail. "Did someone call my name?"

"Ash is having trouble again," Kaitlin told her brother. "Do you have a few minutes to help?"

Troy jumped to the ground. "Going from the ground to a horse is a big change," he told Ashleigh. "But it's not that much more difficult. You've just got to remember that you're five feet up in the air. You need to change your angle to accommodate it."

Ashleigh furrowed her brow in concentration as she spun the rope over her head. She homed in on the steer's horns, concentrating hard on where the rope was going to land. "I did it!" she cried triumphantly as the rope settled over the long horns of the practice steer. But her excitement was short-lived.

A loud clapping sound came from out in the desert. They all turned to see Shelby sitting on her golden palomino out in the sagebrush.

"Great job, kid," Shelby said with a laugh. "It only took you seven tries this time."

Troy gave Shelby a dirty look. "Don't you have something better to do? Small furry animals to scare or something?"

Shelby laughed and flipped her long blond hair over

her shoulder. "I'm just here to see how the competition is doing. I guess I don't have to worry about the roping events," she said snidely.

Troy patted Flash on the haunches and smiled. "But you *will* have to worry about the running events, Shel. I've been watching Ashleigh, and I think she'll beat you in a few of those."

Shelby reined her mare in a sharp half turn. "Yeah, right," she scoffed over her shoulder as she rode away. "Like that's really going to happen. I'm shaking all the way down to my cowboy boots."

Ashleigh watched the girl disappear over the hill, reminding herself that the contest with Shelby wasn't that important. "Has she always been that mean?" she asked.

Kaitlin nodded. "For as long as I can remember."

Ashleigh dismounted and gave Flash a pat. "Let's forget about Shelby," she suggested. "I've got some ideas that might help Ranger's training. Winning a race is a lot more important than tossing a rope over the horns of a stupid steer," she said with a laugh. But as she hooked her rope back over the fence post, she remembered the satisfaction she had felt at settling the rope over her target.

Ashleigh smiled. It wasn't as good as winning a race, but it was something fun she could take home to teach her friends.

. . .

At supper that night Jim handed the race book to Kaitlin. "I found another race for Ranger, but this one is a mile."

"Do you think that's too far for him?" Kaitlin said in concern. "This is only his second race, and it's on Friday. That'll give him just five days between races."

Jim filled his plate with fried chicken, mashed potatoes, and fresh green beans. "Ranger was just out for a gallop his last race. He wasn't the least bit tired after the six-furlong race. Maybe the extra quarter mile will help him out," he said hopefully. "His line is bred to run distance."

Linda passed the milk to Kaitlin. "We need to really get serious with Ranger's training this week," she said. "If he runs as poorly this time as he did the last, we're going to have to pull him out of training."

There was silence all around the table.

"But how can you quit on him after only two races?" Kaitlin cried. Ashleigh could tell that she was close to tears.

Jim gave her a sympathetic look. "Kaitlin, Ranger showed no promise whatsoever in his first start." He paused for a long moment, as if considering how to make his words less painful. "Honey, he wasn't even close. If he runs the same race and shows no desire to compete, we don't have the money to keep him in training. We need to sell him for a riding horse and get something that will run."

Ashleigh knew how much Kaitlin loved Ranger. She felt horrible for her cousin. It would mean a lot to Kaitlin to see the gelding succeed.

Kaitlin pushed her plate away. "I don't feel very hungry. May I be excused?" she asked as she stared at her lap.

Her parents exchanged worried glances. Linda nodded. "Sure, Kaitlin. I'll keep your plate warm for later in case you change your mind."

Ashleigh flinched at the loud banging of the screen as Kaitlin raced out the back door to be with her horse. She pushed the mashed potatoes around on her plate. Suddenly her appetite was gone, too.

"She'll be okay," Troy said reassuringly. "Kaitlin just needs to cool off and think about this. In her heart she knows Mom and Dad are right about the racing part."

"Oh, Ashleigh," Linda said. "I forgot to tell you that there's a message on the machine for you. It's from your friend Mona. She said something about somebody riding your horse. Don't forget to get it after supper."

"Thank you," Ashleigh said as she pushed her potatoes around some more. She wondered about the message. She knew that Mona was riding Stardust. That must have been what Linda meant.

Ashleigh took several bites from a chicken leg. She knew she wouldn't be excused from the table until it looked as though she had eaten her fill. She finished the chicken and a few bites of green beans, then pushed her chair back. "Excuse me. I think I'll go get that message," she said.

When she hit the playback button, Ashleigh was surprised to hear the concern in Mona's voice.

"I caught Rory sneaking a ride on Stardust today," the message began. "He coaxed her over to the fence and hopped on her back. I had a talk with your parents about it, and he got into trouble. But I think Rory wants to trade in his pony for your mare."

The answering machine beeped, indicating the end of the message. Ashleigh sat down on the overstuffed chair, not sure what to think. Rory couldn't take over her horse—her parents wouldn't allow it. He was obviously too small for Stardust. But still, the thought of Rory getting cozy with her mare made her feel a little uneasy.

She stood and walked to the door, planning to join her cousin in the barn. Things had been rough for both of them the last several days. They needed a little luck to come their way.

•   •   •

Race day, Friday, came awfully fast. Ashleigh's cousins had taken some of her suggestions about Ranger, but the gelding still seemed disinterested in training.

"Hand me that hoof pick, would you, Ash?" Kaitlin said as she bent over Ranger's hoof.

Ashleigh grabbed the pick and handed it to her cousin, then continued to run the soft brush over Ranger's coat to bring out the shine. "There's the call to the gate," Ashleigh said as a man's voice came over the PA system. "Let's get the drench gun and rinse out his mouth. Your dad said the pony horse is here to lead Ranger over to the front side."

Ashleigh noticed that her cousin's hands were shaking as she filled the drench gun with water. "He's going to do fine, Kate," she reassured. "He had a couple of good long gallops this past week. Ranger is ready for this mile."

Kaitlin inserted the drench gun in the side of Ranger's mouth and pushed the plunger, sending a cascade of water over the horse's tongue to wash out any hay or straw that had stuck in there. When she was done, she tossed the drench gun back in the bucket. "He's got to do well this time, Ash," she said as she threw her arms around Ranger's neck and buried her face in his mane. "If he doesn't, my parents will take him out of training and sell him."

"Let's go, Kaitlin!" Linda shouted from the end of the shed row. "You're going to miss your race if you don't hurry."

Kaitlin grabbed Ranger's reins and led him out of the stall. She handed him off to the pony rider and followed behind with the rest of the Gilbert gang.

When they got to the front side, Ashleigh and Kaitlin stood outside the saddling ring and watched as Ranger was saddled and then circled for the betting crowd to view. When the jockeys came out to mount up, Ashleigh was glad to see that they had a new rider aboard Ranger. Maybe this one would do a better job getting Ranger to get up and go.

But as they watched the little bay gelding trot along in the post parade, Ashleigh began to experience some of Kaitlin's worries herself. Ranger played around, nipping at the pony horse's shoulder and shaking his head as he played with the bit. His mind didn't seem to be on business.

They finished the parade for the crowd and cantered off to warm up the horses. Ashleigh and Kaitlin found a spot beside Troy on the rail directly in front of the starting gate. Since this was a half-mile track and the race was a mile, the horses would start at the finish line and circle the track twice.

Jim and Linda joined them on the rail. "We've got

the perfect spot," Linda said. "We'll get to see Ranger break from the gate, and we'll be right here when he runs across the line first."

Kaitlin smiled at her mother, but Ashleigh could tell that her cousin was leery about sharing her mother's optimism. The horses returned, and the gate crew began loading them into the chutes. Ranger had drawn the number four hole. When his turn came, he balked at the gate, refusing to enter.

"Come on, Ranger," Kaitlin whispered. "Quit clowning around."

As if he had heard his owner's plea, Ranger stepped forward into the gate, and the doors locked closed behind him. He pawed at the ground and blew through his lips as if he was anxious to be off. But when all the horses were loaded and the starting gate clanged open, the little bay broke slowly from the gate and ended up many lengths behind the last horse.

"Come on, Ranger, move up!" Kaitlin cried. But as the horses passed the finish line for the first lap of the track, Ranger remained in his last-place position.

Jim and Linda exchanged worried glances, and Troy was yelling himself hoarse as he banged on the rail. Ashleigh was glad that he seemed to know how important this was to Kaitlin and was trying to help.

"Lone Star is in the lead, with Right Choice running

second and Kiss Me Kate in third!" the announcer called. "Bold Ranger is the last horse in the field by fifteen lengths."

Kaitlin closed her eyes and leaned on the rail. "This is too horrible. I can't even watch."

The horses pounded down the backside of the track, heading for the turn that would lead to the homestretch.

"He's moving up!" Ashleigh cried as she watched Ranger gain ground in the turn. She wasn't sure if Ranger was gaining or the other horses were beginning to fade. Either way, he was now only five lengths behind the last horse.

Kaitlin opened her eyes and stood on her toes. "Come on, Ranger!" She jumped up and down, shouting her encouragement.

"They're coming down the homestretch, and it's Right Choice taking the lead, with Kiss Me Kate running second and Lone Star fading back in the pack!" the announcer called excitedly. "Bold Ranger continues to pull up the rear, but he's closed the gap to a length. They pass the finish line, and Right Choice is the winner of this mile race!"

Ashleigh watched helplessly as Kaitlin's hopes folded like a collapsing chair. Ranger had run dead last again, and now his fate was sealed.

9

The ride home from the track was deathly quiet. Kaitlin seemed to fall asleep with her head resting against the truck's window, but Ashleigh had the suspicion that her cousin was faking sleep so she wouldn't have to deal with the discussion of Ranger and how he was to be made into a saddle horse and be put up for sale.

Ashleigh leaned her head back and closed her eyes. The hum of the tires on the road as they rolled down the highway lulled her to sleep. She woke when they pulled into the Gilberts' stable yard.

"Come on, Kaitlin. We're home," Ashleigh said as they climbed from the truck.

Linda closed the door on the vehicle and turned to Ashleigh and Kaitlin. "You two take care of Ranger while Troy and Jim do the feeding. I'll go up and get dinner started."

Ashleigh opened the trailer door while Kaitlin untied Ranger and backed him from the trailer. They gave him a good brushing and rubbed his legs with a strong liniment, then turned him loose in his stall.

Kaitlin closed the door and leaned against it, staring at Ranger as he dropped to his knees to roll in the fresh straw. "What am I going to do, Ash?" she said in desperation. "I can't let them sell Ranger as a saddle horse. I know he can win if they just give him a little more time. You've got to help me," she cried. "We've got to save Ranger from being sold!"

Ashleigh bobbed her head in agreement. "Of course I'll help," she said. "We'll figure something out. Although I don't think now would be a good time to ask your parents about keeping Ranger. They might not want to run him again, but I think we can at least talk them into letting you keep him as a riding horse."

Kaitlin fed Ranger a piece of apple she had saved from her lunch. "Tony is getting pretty old and slow. He's going to need to be retired pretty soon. Maybe my parents will let me keep Ranger as a replacement. But I know he could win at the track, Ash. He just needs another chance."

Troy peeked his head out the tack room door. "Are you girls still going to the gymkhana tomorrow?" he asked.

Kaitlin shrugged. "I don't know. With all the problems with Ranger, I don't really feel like going to the show tomorrow."

Ashleigh frowned. "You've been looking forward to this since I first got here," she said to Kaitlin. "You've got to go. Maybe it will help take your mind off of Ranger."

"You should probably load all your equipment in the trailer tonight," Troy suggested. "That'll save you some extra time in the morning."

Ashleigh looked at her cousin with sympathy. "While you're competing tomorrow, I'll be trying to figure out a plan to save Ranger."

Kaitlin motioned for Ashleigh to follow her to the tack room. She got out two saddles and two bridles.

"Oh, no," Ashleigh said, lifting her hands in protest. "I'm not ready to compete tomorrow."

"Come on, Ash," Kaitlin cajoled. "I think it would be a good idea for you to ride in a class or two."

Ashleigh shook her head in protest. "I'm not ready."

Kaitlin handed the extra tack to Ashleigh to load in the trailer. "You're more ready than you think," she said. "Just take Flash and ride around the grounds for the first few classes so you can see how everything works. You can enter the pole-bending or barrel class." She paused and gave Ashleigh an exasperated look. "You're too serious about winning, Ash. Sometimes it's okay just to go and have fun."

Ashleigh hesitated for a moment. Her cousin was right. Hadn't she just been telling herself that she needed to forget about competing with Shelby? It would be good to be able to see all of the events in person. "Okay," she said reluctantly. "Maybe I can ride in one of the classes just to get the feel of it."

Kaitlin sighed. "I might not even compete in all the classes tomorrow," she said. "I need to put all of my concentration into figuring out a way to keep Ranger and get him back to the races again."

"Don't worry, Kate," Ashleigh said. "We'll work on that one together. I promise!"

The gymkhana show was a lot more fun than Ashleigh had expected. Kaitlin rode in only a few classes, but she won two of them and placed well in another. Shelby Jeffrey also did her fair share of winning. With each ribbon she received, she made sure she paraded it past Ashleigh and Kaitlin, no matter where they were standing.

Ashleigh entered Flash in the pole-bending contest. It was a class that Shelby wasn't riding in. Ashleigh was surprised to see how badly her hands were shaking as she rode up to the line, waiting to make her run. Unfortunately, she passed that nervousness to her horse, and Flash began to dance in place and toss her head.

When Ashleigh gave the mare the signal to go, Flash charged toward the poles, missing the first two before she began her in-and-out weave down through the line.

"Easy, mare," Ashleigh crooned, trying to keep her voice steady in order to quiet the eager paint. Flash eased up on her headlong flight and settled into a good cadence, but it was too late. They had already missed the first two poles and knocked over another.

Ashleigh gave the mare a pat as they exited the arena. It wasn't Flash's fault that they had run so poorly. Kaitlin had been right. She'd needed the practice run to see just how badly things could go. Ashleigh made up her mind then and there. It would be fun to beat Shelby, but the important thing was to do the best she could for herself and her horse. Winning wasn't everything.

At noon they loaded the horses up and went home.

"When are you going to start schooling Ranger to be a trail horse?" Linda asked as she pulled from the arena parking lot.

Kaitlin flinched at the question, but she looked to Ashleigh for support before she answered. "There's no reason we can't start today after lunch," she said.

Linda cut down the back roads that led to their ranch. "Your brother says that Ranger will be safe for you to ride, but just the same, I'd like you to ride him in the round pen for a bit before you take him out on the trails." She turned to Ashleigh. "I think it would be a good idea if you ponied Kaitlin and Ranger for a few miles on the trails just to make sure he's going to be okay."

Ashleigh nodded in agreement, but she didn't think her cousin had anything to worry about. Ranger didn't even want to run off during a race. She doubted he would attempt it on the trail.

They reached the ranch, and Ashleigh and Kaitlin took care of the two mares while Troy saddled Ranger and ran him around the pen.

"I can't get over how you guys ride a horse the next day after his race," Ashleigh said as she put her English saddle on the Arabian mare. "Our trainer friend at Edgardale waits at least three days after a race before he'll put a horse back on the track."

Kaitlin laughed. "In case you haven't noticed, Ash, you're not at Edgardale," she teased. "Besides, Ranger barely cracked a sweat from his last race. It wasn't any different for him than a regular gallop."

They went to the round pen, where Ranger stood waiting for them. Kaitlin put her foot in the stirrup and mounted up. She rode Ranger for several laps at a trot and a slow canter. Finally Troy declared them ready to go.

Ashleigh attached a lead rope to Ranger's halter as the gelding and Kaitlin came through the gate. Ariel snorted and stepped backward, almost jerking Ashleigh from the saddle. "This might not be such a great idea," Ashleigh said as she cued the mare hard with her legs, forcing the Arabian to step forward and walk beside Ranger.

Tony grabbed the mare's bit and walked with them to the trailhead. "If Ariel keeps acting up, turn Ranger loose," Troy instructed. "I'm sure Ranger is going to be fine. There's no use in both of you getting hurt. This mare can get a little crazy."

Ashleigh kept the lead line on Ranger until the trail narrowed. She turned Ranger loose, and the two girls moved single file down the sandy path, with herself and Ariel in the lead. The mare spooked at several large rocks along the path.

"What's the matter with this horse?" Ashleigh said in aggravation. "I'm sure you guys have ridden her down this trail a hundred times."

"At least a hundred," Kaitlin said with a chuckle. "She's just a spooky mare. Most Arabians are pretty high-strung. Why don't we ask for a trot and get some of her energy out?"

Ashleigh grabbed a big handful of mane and asked the mare to move out. She continued to spook, but at least Ashleigh now knew that the rocks bothered her, and she could prepare for the mare to jump sideways. "How's Ranger doing?" Ashleigh asked as she turned to give a quick look at Kaitlin and her horse. Ranger was bobbing his head and chewing at the bit, playing like a young colt on one of his first rides.

"He's behaving okay, except for this head-bobbing thing," Kaitlin replied. "Ranger doesn't ever seem to want to get serious about anything."

They continued at the trot for several miles. Ashleigh was amazed at the stamina the Arabian mare had. She looked back several times to see how her cousin was doing with Ranger. After the third mile the gelding began to perspire, and he stopped bobbing his head and started to concentrate on the ride. "Ranger still okay?" Ashleigh called back over her shoulder.

"We're fine," Kaitlin replied. "He still has plenty of energy left. He's just having to work a little bit now."

They continued on, taking a trail that went up a series of small hills. When they reached the top, Ashleigh pulled her mare to a halt to admire the beautiful view. She took a deep breath of the fresh desert air and wondered how she ever could have thought that Nevada was a bland-looking place.

The valley below stretched out with a mixture of pale green sagebrush, pink flowering desert peach, and bitterbrush with its tiny yellow flowers. A few pinyon pines grew here and there, stretching their scraggly branches toward the brilliant blue sky. The tan sand made the vibrantly colored desert flowers stand out even more.

A movement in the valley caught Ashleigh's eye. "Look!" she cried. "Mustangs!"

Kaitlin pulled Ranger up beside Ariel. The gelding was sweating and blowing, but he didn't seem to be too tired. "Let's follow them," Kaitlin said.

They carefully picked their way down the hillside. When they reached the valley floor, they walked their horses toward the herd of wild mustangs, trying to get as close as possible before the herd took flight.

"This band is different from the one we saw yesterday," Ashleigh observed. "Most of these horses are light-colored."

Kaitlin smiled knowingly. "I call this herd the sunshine bunch," she said. "You notice that most of the mares are palominos, buckskins, and duns. This stallion has a fondness for light-colored mares. He won't accept a bay or a black."

"That's pretty unusual, isn't it?" Ashleigh asked as she steered Ariel down another path that would lead to the herd. "I didn't know horses were picky."

Kaitlin nodded. "You don't see it very often, but some stallions are particular. I've even seen that buckskin stallion raid another herd and run off with the palominos and duns."

"Wow," Ashleigh said dreamily. "It sure would be neat to own one of those horses."

"The Bureau of Land Management does roundups a few times a year, when they determine that there's not enough forage to support the growing herds," Kaitlin explained. "You can adopt the horses for one hundred twenty-five dollars."

Ashleigh turned in the saddle. "That's all?"

"Yup," Kaitlin said. "Plus there are a few rules to follow. You have to be at least eighteen years old, but your parents can adopt the horse and allow you to be the main caretaker. And you have to have a six-foot fence to keep them in."

Ashleigh brushed her hair out of her eyes, keeping a watch on the wild herd. "That would be so awesome!" she said. "But I live in Kentucky. That would be too far for my parents to haul."

"Maybe not," Kaitlin said. "Sometimes the BLM hauls truckloads of mustangs back east so that the people back there can have a chance to adopt them."

Ashleigh imagined riding one of the fleet-footed mustangs as she raced over the fields at home. A slight frown came to her face. "It would be really cool to own a mustang, but in a way it's a shame to take them off their land and tame them."

"I know what you mean," Kaitlin agreed. "But the thing is, these horses keep having babies, and there's only so much feed out here. Plus the cattle ranchers have been battling with the mustangs for a long time," she explained. "They need what little grass is out here to feed their cattle for the market. They'd be happy if all the mustangs were taken off the land and they had it all to themselves. So, to keep things in balance, some of the mustangs are captured and put up for adoption. Otherwise they'd starve."

Ashleigh rode in silence for a few minutes, keeping her eyes on the beautiful mustangs. She couldn't imagine the noble creatures starving to death. When she got home, she'd ask her parents about adopting a mustang if they ever came to her area.

"They've spotted us," Kaitlin said as she pointed to the buckskin stallion, who had moved out to challenge them. "Hold here for a minute and let's see what they do."

The stallion arched his neck until his black mane bristled, and he shook his small, Arabian-like head while he neighed a challenge. He pawed the earth and snorted. When he saw that they were no threat, he gathered his mares and moved them off at a gallop.

"Let's follow!" Ashleigh said.

They bumped their horses into a gallop and followed the herd at a safe distance.

Ashleigh laughed with glee as the Arabian mare cocked her tail over her back and galloped after the wild horses as though she were part of the herd. The warm breeze rushed through Ashleigh's hair as they dodged through the sagebrush, racing with the wind. When they reached the end of the short valley, the mustangs took one of their special trails up into their mountain hideouts, and the girls pulled their horses to a stop.

Ashleigh could feel the warmth of her flushed cheeks as the blood pounded through her veins. "That was incredible!" she cried. "I felt like I was a part of the herd!"

Kaitlin swept her long dark hair out of her eyes and laughed. "Tell me you'll ever do anything like *that* in Kentucky!"

Ashleigh watched the cloud of dust rise into the air and disappear. Looking at the valley now, no one would ever guess the wild ones had just been there.

Kaitlin glanced at her watch. "We'd better get home."

They turned the horses and headed back to the ranch. They had ridden a long way that day, and they had miles to go before they'd be home.

"Ariel is still full of oats," Ashleigh said. "How is Ranger holding out?"

Kaitlin patted the gelding's neck. "He's sweaty, but he seems to be doing pretty well."

Ashleigh studied the little bay gelding for several moments. "You know, Kate, this kind of training may be what Ranger needs. This is the first time I've seen him be serious about a workout," she said. "Maybe if we do this kind of ride a couple of times a week, he might be able to do better at the track."

Kaitlin's face lifted in hope. "Do you really think so?"

Ashleigh nodded. "It's just too bad that they don't have any five-mile races," she said with a chuckle. "He'd beat them by a mile!"

"That's it!" Kaitlin said, her voice full of excitement. "The meet we've been racing at ends in three weeks. There's a two-mile race on the last day. It's a really big deal, and everyone comes to watch."

"Two miles?" Ashleigh gasped. "The Belmont Stakes is a mile and a half, and that's the longest race I've ever heard of."

"I bet Ranger could do it," Kaitlin said. "That's our only hope. That two-mile race is what's going to save Ranger!"

"I think you're right," Ashleigh agreed. "Your father said that Ranger is bred for distance. After the way he traveled today, I bet he could run that two-mile race. All he'd have to do is pick a good pace and stay at it while the other horses burn themselves out and fall back."

Kaitlin's face fell. "But how are we going to talk my parents into that when they said Ranger will never set foot on the track again?"

Ashleigh scrunched her brows and thought. "I think

we should keep training Ranger, and a week before the race we'll tell your parents what we've been doing and ask for another chance. Maybe they'll see the improvement in his attitude and agree."

Kaitlin smiled broadly. "I'm so glad you came to visit, Ash. Not only have we had a bunch of fun, but I wouldn't be able to do this without you. You're the best!"

They asked their horses for a trot and wound their way through the sagebrush toward home. It took them an hour to reach the ranch. Everyone was out doing the evening chores when they arrived.

"Wow, it looks like you had quite a ride," Troy said when they rode up to the hitching post and dismounted. "You'd better give both of those horses a bath and a good rubdown."

Kaitlin pulled the saddle from Ranger's back. "Could you put an extra helping of oats in each of their stalls for me, Troy?"

Troy nodded, then handed Ashleigh the wash bucket and scraper. "We're almost done here. Dad's grilling steaks for dinner tonight. You girls had better hurry or I'm going to eat your share!"

Kaitlin turned the hose on her brother, giving him a good dousing as he ran for the house, laughing as he went. "That does it, Kate," he warned. "I'm definitely eating your dinner!"

Ashleigh watched the teasing banter between Kaitlin and Troy and thought about her own brother and sister. She turned away before another bout of homesickness came on. She was having a great time here with her cousins. She didn't want to wreck it.

When the horses were finished and turned into their paddocks, the girls made their way to the house.

"Go wash up," Kaitlin's mom warned. "I can smell the horse on you from here. Dinner will be ready in ten minutes."

Ashleigh started to make her way to the bathroom, but she stopped when Linda called to her.

"Ashleigh, there's a letter that came from your folks today," Linda said as she set a big plate of watermelon on the counter.

"A letter?" Ashleigh asked in surprise. Why would her parents send her a letter when it was so easy to call?

"What is it, Ash?" Kaitlin said as she watched Ashleigh open the long white envelope.

Ashleigh unfolded the papers inside and stared at them for several moments before she understood what she was looking at. Her heart jumped, and she gasped as she realized the meaning of what she was reading. Then the papers fell from her fingers, landing in a pile on the floor.

10

"What's the matter, Ash?" Kaitlin cried in alarm.

"It's St-Stardust," Ashleigh stammered. She dropped to the floor and gathered the papers, making sure she had read them correctly. "It's no wonder she was gaining weight. Stardust is going to have a foal!"

"That's great, Ashleigh!" Jim and Linda chorused, and Troy raised his glass in salute.

Kaitlin wrinkled her brow. "But I didn't know Stardust had been bred," she said in confusion. "Why didn't you tell me about that?"

Ashleigh explained about the accidental breeding to Royal Renegade that had happened in the spring.

"Didn't you check Stardust to see if she was in foal?" Troy said as he gathered the fresh corn on the cob to put on the grill. He shouldered the back door open and paused, waiting for her answer.

Ashleigh shrugged. "She came back in season. There was no reason to suspect that she was in foal."

Jim nodded. "I've heard of that happening. It's kind of rare, but some mares act like they're in season even though they're in foal."

Kaitlin slapped Ashleigh a high five. "Congratulations!" she said. "I'm sure Stardust will have a beautiful foal."

Linda grabbed the bottles of soda from the refrigerator. "We're eating outside tonight," she said. "Let's celebrate Ashleigh's good fortune with a steak dinner!"

They laughed and talked through the dinner, telling tales of horses that had raced or had gone on to greatness in another event. Ashleigh wondered what she would do with Stardust's foal. It wasn't a purebred, so it couldn't race, but she was sure she could train it to do dressage or jumping. The more she thought about it, the more excited she got.

Ashleigh pushed the remaining food around on her plate as she glanced sideways at Kaitlin. She had a little more than three weeks of vacation left, but Stardust needed her now. Would Kaitlin mind if she went home early? They had already figured out a plan of action for Ranger. All her cousin had to do was carry it out. Surely Kaitlin would understand how important it was for Ashleigh to return to Edgardale.

When dinner was over, Ashleigh helped Kaitlin carry the plates back into the house. As she stacked the dishes near the sink, she glanced at a magazine that pictured a mare and foal on the cover. She had to tell her cousin about her change of plans. "I'm going to call my parents tonight and see if I can come home early," Ashleigh said.

Kaitlin stopped in her tracks and whirled to face Ashleigh. "Go home early?" she said in dismay. "How early?"

Ashleigh set the plates in the sink and shrugged. "I don't know. It'll probably take a couple of days to get the ticket changed."

Kaitlin set the plates down with a thump. "A couple of days?" she squeaked.

Ashleigh nodded dreamily. "Just a few more days and I can be home with Stardust, getting her prepared to have a foal."

"But what about your promise to me and Ranger?" Kaitlin cried. "You promised to help us, and now you're going to go back on your promise? Stardust won't have that foal until next spring! Why do you need to go home now?"

Ashleigh rinsed the plates and set them in the dishwasher. "There's so many things that can go wrong when a mare is in foal," Ashleigh said. "I just want to make sure that Stardust has the best care possible. I know my parents will look after her, but they've got all the other mares to take care of. I can give Stardust all the extra care she needs."

"But you promised," Kaitlin cried.

Ashleigh bit her bottom lip. Her cousin wasn't taking this very well. "I'm sure Troy will help," Ashleigh said, but she could see from the expression on Kaitlin's face that that wasn't what she wanted to hear.

Kaitlin took a deep breath and angrily brushed at the tears that were forming in her eyes. "How could you desert me like this?" she accused. "You said you would help me get Ranger back to the races."

Ashleigh crossed her arms and stared at her cousin. Why didn't Kaitlin understand? Stardust was in foal! That was the best thing that could happen. She had to go home to be with her horse. "You'll be okay, Kate," she said. "Ranger did really well today. If you keep training him like that, he'll do fine."

Kaitlin put her hands on her hips. "My parents won't let me ride Ranger out into the desert by myself," she said. "And I know Troy won't go with me. You're our only hope, Ash, but you're thinking only of yourself!" She ran out the door, letting it slam after her.

Linda entered the room, her arms loaded with leftovers. "What's wrong with Kaitlin?" she asked. "She was laughing just a minute ago."

Ashleigh crammed her hands into her pockets and

129

stared at the floor. "We had a little fight," she admitted. "I think Kaitlin went out to be with her horse."

Linda put the ketchup and steak sauce back into the refrigerator. "I'm sure it'll blow over. You girls have been together an awful lot lately. Maybe she just needs a few minutes to herself."

Ashleigh nodded, but she knew it went deeper than that. Part of her felt guilty for betraying her cousin and backing out on a promise, but Stardust being in foal was her dream come true. She needed to get home as soon as possible. "Can I call my parents again?" she asked Linda.

Linda nodded, picked up the phone, and dialed the number, then handed it to Ashleigh. The phone rang three times before her mother picked it up.

"Hi, Mom, it's me," Ashleigh said.

"I bet I know what you're calling about," Mrs. Griffen said with a chuckle.

Ashleigh bombarded her mother with questions about Stardust and the pending foal. When her mother finished answering all the questions, Ashleigh asked the tough one. "Mom, I'd like to come home as soon as possible. Can you and Dad get my ticket changed?"

There was an unexpected silence on the other end of the line as Ashleigh waited for her mother's reply.

"You don't need to come home yet, Ashleigh," Mrs.

Griffen said. "There's nothing you can do here for Stardust. She's only about three months along. Stay and enjoy the rest of your vacation," she advised.

"But I want to come home," she insisted.

There was another long pause, and then Mrs. Griffen spoke. "Aren't you and Kaitlin having a good time?"

"We're having a great time," Ashleigh said. "It's just that I think I should be home in case Stardust needs me."

Mrs. Griffen sighed. "I don't think your father is going to be pleased, Ash," she said in a serious tone. "It's going to cost a lot of money to change the ticket, and there's no emergency here. I'll speak to your dad and get back to you."

Ashleigh said goodbye and hung up the phone. She looked out the window toward the barn. It was almost dark, but she could see Kaitlin standing in the pen with Ranger. She needed to go to her cousin and make her understand why it was so important for her to return to Edgardale.

She slipped out the back door and made her way to the barnyard. Kaitlin was standing with her arms around Ranger's neck, and Ashleigh could hear her crying from where she stood. "Kaitlin?" she called softly. She waited for several moments and was about to call Kaitlin's name again when she heard her cousin's choked response.

"What do you want?" Kaitlin dropped her arms and turned to face Ashleigh.

Ashleigh took a step back, surprised by the anger in her cousin's voice.

"I just wanted you to understand why it's so important that I go home right away," Ashleigh said.

Kaitlin turned her back again. "Just go, Ashleigh," she said with a sob.

Ashleigh took several steps to close the distance between them. "I don't want us to fight, Kaitlin. Can't you understand how exciting this is for me?" she pleaded. "That's why I need to go home now. I really want this foal, Kaitlin. It's a miracle. Like a dream come true."

Kaitlin sighed in frustration. "But don't *you* understand?" she said softly as she wiped the tears from her cheeks. "You're getting your dream. But if you leave now, I'll lose mine."

Ashleigh was stunned. She hadn't thought of it that way. She felt a jolt of shame pass over her. She had been so busy thinking about herself and Stardust's foal that she hadn't really taken into consideration what this would mean to Kaitlin and Ranger. And she'd made a promise to her cousin. Her parents had always told her how important it was for her to keep her word. How easily she had cast it aside when it was inconvenient for her to follow through on it.

Ashleigh felt the tears burning the backs of her eyes. She tilted her head to look at the rising moon, trying to get the tears to go away. "I'm really sorry, Kaitlin," she said in a voice that was barely above a whisper. "I've been a real bonehead, and I was only thinking of myself. I'll keep my promise and stay to help you with Ranger."

Kaitlin's head snapped up. "Are you sure?"

Ashleigh nodded. "My mom was right. There's nothing I could do for Stardust right now, anyway."

Kaitlin gave Ashleigh a hug. "I'm really sorry, too," she apologized. "I know how important Stardust is to you. I shouldn't have thrown such a fit when you said you were leaving." She put her hand out. "Pals?"

Ashleigh grasped her cousin's hand with her own. "Pals!" she said with a smile.

Kaitlin gave Ranger a loving pat and then followed Ashleigh out the gate and back to the house.

"Tomorrow we'll get back to work on Ranger," Ashleigh said. "In a couple of weeks, when he's really fit, we'll ask your parents for another chance."

"Ranger won't let us down, Ash," Kaitlin said as she jerked open the squeaky back door. "He'll make you proud that you decided to stay."

Several days later Ashleigh and Kaitlin had the horses back on the mustang trails. There were no mustangs in sight that day, but manure and fresh tracks showed that they had recently passed through the area.

"Ariel has been behaving pretty well lately," Ashleigh said as she turned in the saddle to see how Kaitlin was doing with Ranger.

Kaitlin posted in time to Ranger's trot, keeping her eyes on the trail to make sure they were traveling on good footing. "Don't let that mare fool you, Ash," Kaitlin warned. "You never want to fall asleep on Ariel, or you might find yourself walking back to the ranch on foot."

"Maybe all of this constant riding is wearing her out," Ashleigh joked. She glanced over at Ranger as he bowed his head and surged forward through the deep sand. "He seems to be doing much better," Ashleigh said. "The other horses in that two-mile race had better watch out!"

They reached the top of the hill and turned around, stopping for a moment to enjoy the view. Two golden eagles flew low over the valley looking for mice or lizards, and a couple of mule deer grazed quietly on the other side. Ashleigh closed her eyes, trying to commit all of this to memory. In a few short weeks she would be back in Kentucky, and she was going to miss this place and her cousins terribly.

They walked the horses down the steep part of the mountain, giving them a chance to blow before they picked up the trot again. When they hit the lower trails, they stepped up the pace.

Ashleigh counted the two-beat gait of the trot as they moved along the trail. *One, two, one, two* . . . She felt her mind wander as she fell under the spell of the lazy afternoon. She didn't pick up on the fact that Ariel had pricked her ears until it was almost too late.

There was a strange rattling sound, and Kaitlin shouted in alarm. Then suddenly the little Arabian mare propped hard and bolted to the side. Ashleigh felt herself slipping from the saddle as her feet came out of the irons. She tried to grab a handful of mane to right herself, but Ariel kept bolting away from the strange noise.

Ashleigh landed on her backside in the deep sand. The air rushed from her lungs, and she gasped for a breath. She was about to stand and run after her horse when she saw the thing that had caused Ariel to spook.

The hair on the back of Ashleigh's neck stood on end, and it felt as though cold water was running through her veins. The slow, eerie shake of the snake's tail held Ashleigh mesmerized as she stared at the largest rattlesnake she had ever seen.

11

"Don't move an inch," Kaitlin whispered, loud enough for Ashleigh to hear her but low enough that it wouldn't upset the snake. "Don't even breathe."

Ashleigh could feel rivulets of sweat running down her forehead and drenching her T-shirt. She knew it was at least ninety degrees out, but she felt cold all over.

The rattler continued the slow shake of its tail. Ranger backed away from the sound, and the snake increased the speed and volume of the rattle at the sudden movement of the horse.

Ashleigh was sure it was a sound she would remember for the rest of her life. It sounded like a paper cup with a handful of beads being shaken with a very deadly intent.

She watched as the brown snake with the wide diamonds on its back moved its wide, flat head to a high striking position. Its tongue flicked in and out of its mouth as it tried to get her scent. Goose bumps rose on her arms.

Ashleigh didn't dare move. She rolled her eyes around to see where Kaitlin was. She could see her cousin and Ranger standing at the edge of her vision.

"I'm going to try something, Ash," Kaitlin said in a low monotone. "If this fails and the snake doesn't slide into the brush, you'd better run as fast as you can in the opposite direction."

Ashleigh didn't have time to ask questions or protest. Kaitlin rushed forward on Ranger, bringing her legs down hard onto the reluctant gelding's sides to get him to move forward. The startled horse made a big lunge toward the rattler, then stopped hard, sending sand flying in all directions. Kaitlin hung on to her saddle horn to keep from going over Ranger's head.

Ashleigh screamed as she scrambled in the sand, never taking her eyes off the snake as she flailed about, trying to gain her feet. She saw the rattler uncoil and strike at Ranger's front legs, but the snake fell short.

She finally gained her footing and turned to run, but she fell into a large sagebrush bush and ended up in the sand once more. She felt the sting of several cuts as her sweat washed into the scrapes she had received from the bush.

"Ashleigh, it's okay," Kaitlin cried. "We scared off the snake—it went into the other bush."

Ashleigh stopped and turned, seeing Kaitlin still mounted on Ranger as they walked toward her. "Are you sure it's gone?" she said as she eyed all the nearby bushes, listening for the unmistakable sound of a rattlesnake's tail. She rubbed at her arms, trying to make the goose bumps go away.

Kaitlin got down off her horse. "I've got to see if Ranger got bitten," she said as she knelt in the sand and inspected the gelding's front legs.

Ashleigh joined her. "I saw the snake strike, but it fell a couple inches short of Ranger's legs."

"Thank goodness!" Kaitlin cried. "I was so afraid Ranger was going to get hurt."

Ashleigh's eyebrows rose. "Then why did you do that?" she asked. "I thought you were crazy when you rode right toward that snake. You could have been thrown, just like I was," Ashleigh scolded.

Kaitlin patted Ranger's neck. "I had a good hold on the saddle," she said. "I knew I wasn't going to come off. I was hoping that the snake would be scared enough to slither off into the bushes."

"But the rattler struck," Ashleigh said. "What if Ranger had been bitten?"

Kaitlin shrugged. "It was a chance I had to take. Horses have poor circulation below their knees," she explained. "If Ranger had been bitten, he'd probably have gotten pretty sick, but he wouldn't have died."

Ashleigh stood silent for a moment, looking at Kaitlin in amazement. Finally she spoke. "You risked yourself and Ranger for me."

Kaitlin kicked at the sand beneath her boots. "You'd have done the same for me," she muttered.

Ashleigh laughed. "I might have wanted to, but I was so scared, I didn't think I was going to be able to move."

"Come on," Kaitlin said as she gathered Ranger's reins. "Ariel's about a hundred yards out, cropping that small patch of bunch grass. Let's go home."

They caught the Arabian mare and mounted up. The ride home was at a more leisurely pace. Ashleigh kept her eyes glued to the sides of the trail, looking for snakes.

"Don't worry, Ash. We probably won't run into any more rattlers," Kaitlin assured her. "Most of the time you don't see the snakes because they hear you coming and disappear into the brush. We just took that one by surprise as it was sunning itself."

Ashleigh laughed. "Believe me, I don't think it was half as surprised as I was!"

The ranch came into view, and they slowed the horses to a walk.

"Would you mind if we skipped the gymkhana training today?" Ashleigh asked. "I think I've had enough excitement for one day."

Kaitlin nodded. "But that means we work twice as

long tomorrow," she cautioned. "You had a practice ride. Next weekend I expect you to enter all of your events. I think you might even be able to beat Shelby in a few of them."

Ashleigh's shoulders slumped. "I don't know, Kate. I think I should have called this thing off when Shelby first accepted my challenge. What chance do I have against a real cowgirl?"

Kaitlin leaned over and socked Ashleigh in the arm. "Cowgirl up, cousin! You're as good a rider as Shelby will ever be."

"Cowgirl up?" Ashleigh said in confusion.

"Haven't you ever heard that expression?" Kaitlin grinned. "It's kind of like 'When the going gets tough, the tough get going.' Cowgirls are tough. So cowgirl up, Ash!"

Ashleigh smiled. "You know, after that disastrous run on Flash last week, I kind of decided that it's not so important for me to beat Shelby anymore," she admitted. "I want to do this right and have a good time."

Kaitlin nodded in understanding. "I'm proud of you, Ash," she said. "You see a lot of competitors hurting their horses because they're determined to win at all costs. You and Flash are doing really well. Just go and have a good time. You'll do fine."

They rode into the stable yard and dismounted. "You're right," Ashleigh said. "I know how to ride, and

Flash knows how to run all of the events. We'll make a good team." She gave her cousin a conspiratorial smile. "And if we happen to beat Shelby in a few events, that's even better."

The girls laughed as they untacked their horses and headed for the barn.

But the following weekend, when Ashleigh was waiting to make her first run at pole bending, her confidence was shaky. She was standing by the fence watching Kaitlin compete in the goat-roping contest when Shelby rode up.

"I hear you pulled out of the goat roping," she said.

Ashleigh looked at the bright red lipstick and matching blotches of red on the girl's cheeks. Shelby was only thirteen, and the heavy makeup made her look more like a clown than a rodeo queen.

"What are you smirking at?" Shelby demanded as she tucked a stray piece of her long blond hair back into her hairnet.

"Nothing," Ashleigh replied, and turned back to watch Kaitlin.

"I asked you a question," Shelby said. "Why did you pull out of the goat roping? Still can't twirl a rope?" she asked sarcastically.

Ashleigh watched Kaitlin successfully rope and tie the goat in a good time. She smiled at Shelby, knowing that Kaitlin had beaten the spoiled cowgirl's time. "I can rope, Shelby, but I've only been at it for a month now. I know I'm not good enough in that event to compete, and I'm grown-up enough to admit it." She turned to Kaitlin and gave her a thumbs-up sign. She heard Shelby huff indignantly behind her.

Shelby wheeled her horse, ready to depart, but not before she had another go at Ashleigh. "I'll see you in the other events, unless you chicken out and pull out of those, too. Oh, by the way," Shelby said in an innocent voice, still trying to bait Ashleigh, "you and Kaitlin might want to take a run up to the judges' shack to take a look at the belt buckle that was donated for the winner of the barrel-racing event. It's got my name written all over it!" She laughed as she trotted off.

Kaitlin left the arena and signaled for Ashleigh to follow her back to the horse trailer.

"Great time," Ashleigh said. "You beat Shelby by a whole three seconds."

Kaitlin smiled. "Shelby had a bad run. I think she was concentrating so hard on beating me that she wasn't paying attention to what she was doing. One of these days that's going to get her into trouble." She dismounted and tied Koda to the horse trailer. "Don't fall into the same trap, Ash," Kaitlin warned. "Just go out there and have a good time, the way we discussed."

Ashleigh nodded. She took a deep breath and told herself that this was just a play day. She'd be home soon, and it would be another treasured memory.

"There's the first call for the pole bending," Kaitlin said. "Check Flash's tack and let's go."

Ashleigh checked her saddle and bridle while Kaitlin went to pick up her ribbon for the class. Since it was a jackpot class, Kaitlin would also have some money waiting for her at the end of the day.

The final call for the pole-bending class came, and Ashleigh put on her hat and mounted up.

Shelby was the first to go. She had a great run and came out of the ring with a broad smile on her face. "Beat that one, girls," she said with a tip of her cowboy hat.

Several more people went, and then it was Kaitlin's turn. She ran a good time that was only a fraction slower than Shelby's.

Ashleigh gulped when her name was called. She walked Flash into the ring, making a couple of small circles to calm herself and the anxious mare down. "Easy, girl," she crooned as she tried to steady her own heartbeat. When she was ready, Ashleigh turned Flash in the direction of the poles and pressed her legs to her sides.

Ashleigh's hat flew off as the mare dug in, racing

toward the line of poles. Ashleigh balanced herself as Flash weaved in and out of the white poles, changing leads with ease. They completed the poles and flew across the finish line. Ashleigh could tell by the cheering of the crowd that she had posted a good time. She trotted out of the arena and joined Kaitlin on the fence.

"Way to go, Ash!" Kaitlin said. "You're in second place, right ahead of me." She laughed.

"But I'm still right behind Shelby, right?" Ashleigh stepped down off her horse.

Kaitlin wagged a finger at her. "Remember, this is supposed to be fun. You had a great run. Enjoy it."

"Right," Ashleigh said with a smile. "After we collect our ribbons, let's tie the horses and go look at that belt buckle Shelby was talking about."

The results were called, and they congratulated Shelby on her win as they accepted their own prizes. There was another event before the huddle-scuttle, so Ashleigh and Kaitlin made their way to the judge's shack to look at the buckle.

One look was all it took for Ashleigh to fall in love with the shiny silver prize. The metal was sculpted with the image of a girl and horse going around a barrel. It would make the perfect souvenir to take back to Kentucky.

"Come on, Ash," Kaitlin said as she tugged on

Ashleigh's arm. "It's time to get back to the horses. You're beginning to drool."

Ashleigh grinned as she allowed herself to be led from the building. She didn't care if she didn't place in any other event, but it would be really cool if she could win that belt buckle in the barrel-racing contest.

As the day wore on, it got hotter, and Ashleigh found the long-sleeved Western shirt to be stifling. She placed in several more events and even won the wacky egg-and-spoon race. She sponged Flash off between events, trying to keep her cool so she would be fresh for the barrel event. When the announcer finally called for the barrel-racing contestants, Ashleigh felt her stomach flop.

"Let's go," Kaitlin said as she placed her cowboy hat on her head and mounted up. "This is our last event of the day. Let's make it a good one."

Several other girls went before it was Kaitlin's turn. Ashleigh cheered as her cousin rounded the first barrel in perfect form. Kaitlin was bent low over Koda's withers as she rode hard between the barrels to gain time. She circled the second barrel and charged toward the third. But as Koda went into the last barrel, the mare cut it too short and the barrel tipped, knocking Kaitlin out of the running for the prize.

Shelby was next. Her hat flew off as she charged to the first barrel, and her blond hair waved on the breeze. She rounded the first barrel and made her way to the second with the crowd shouting encouragement. Ashleigh took notes as the cowgirl leaned forward to encourage her horse in the straightaway, then sat her weight back in the saddle to slow the horse for the sharp turn around the barrel. As they approached the last barrel, Shelby's horse floated out a little wide, and the crowd voiced their concern with a sharp intake of breath as Shelby fought to keep the horse in a tight turn, then continued with the run to the finish line.

The crowd cheered again when Shelby's time was posted. Despite the mishap, she had turned in the fastest time of the group.

Ashleigh was the last rider to go. She passed Shelby on the way into the arena. "Nice run," she said.

Shelby gave her a sour look. "I don't need your sarcasm," she snipped. "My horse drifted a bit, but I straightened him out."

"I know," Ashleigh said. "I wasn't being mean. You had a great ride, and you did a really good job of getting your horse back on track. You're a good rider."

Shelby paused for a moment, as if shocked by Ashleigh's words. "Thanks," she mumbled as she pulled off her gloves, seeming to look at Ashleigh in a new light. "Have a good ride," she said.

Ashleigh smiled. Being nice to Shelby had been difficult, but she hadn't been lying when she'd told the girl she had done well. In spite of the small mishap, Shelby had run a great time. It was going to be difficult to beat.

Ashleigh walked Flash for a few strides and then broke her into a trot. She asked the mare for a canter and sped up as they approached the timer. She wanted to be at full speed when they passed the start.

Ashleigh heard the shouts of encouragement as she headed toward the first barrel. She kept her eye on the pocket that she wanted to turn in and balanced herself as Flash whipped around the first barrel and headed for the second.

She lay low over the mare's withers, the way jockeys did in a race, as Flash pounded toward the second blue barrel. As they approached the turn she rebalanced her weight to help her horse make the turn, then jetted toward the final barrel.

Ashleigh concentrated extra hard, knowing that this was where Shelby had made her mistake. She gathered her inside rein and put extra pressure from her outside leg to help Flash around the turn, but it was too late when Ashleigh realized that she had overcorrected her horse.

She felt the hard edge of the barrel on her leg as they made contact during the turn. Ashleigh reached out her hand to steady the tilting barrel as she had seen other riders do, but she didn't have a chance to see if the barrel stayed upright as she came out of the turn and charged toward the finish line.

She scrubbed her reins up and down Flash's neck, encouraging the mare to run her fastest. The cheers of the crowd as she crossed the finish line told Ashleigh that the barrel had stayed upright and that her time had been great. She slowed her mare and looked back over her shoulder at the time clock. She smiled broadly. She had beaten Shelby's time by a fifth of a second. She had won the belt buckle!

12

"Nice ride," Shelby said as she leaned forward in her saddle, extending her hand to Ashleigh.

Ashleigh hesitated for a moment, wondering if this was some kind of a trick that Shelby was playing. When Shelby's hand remained in front of her, Ashleigh reached out and shook it.

"I'm sorry I've been a jerk to you," Shelby apologized. "It's just that this competition stuff gets so fierce, I get carried away sometimes." She pointed to the belt buckle. "That'll be a great souvenir to remind you of your stay here," she said. "You deserved it, Ashleigh. You're a great competitor."

"Thanks," Ashleigh said in surprise as she watched Shelby turn her palomino and walk off.

Kaitlin hollered from outside the arena, "Let's go, Ash. You can shine that new buckle on the way home."

Ashleigh joined her cousin at the trailer and

removed Flash's tack. "One mission accomplished, one to go," she said to Kaitlin as they loaded the horses into the trailer. "I think we should talk to your parents about Ranger tonight."

Kaitlin wrinkled her nose. "Maybe we should wait a few more days."

Ashleigh latched the trailer door and made a final check of the area to make sure they hadn't left any equipment lying around. "A few more days might be too late," she said. "You know your dad. He's going to want to see Ranger work again. If we wait, he's not going to have enough time to enter him in that race."

Kaitlin peeked around the corner of the trailer, making sure her mother wasn't within hearing distance. "Okay, we'll ask them at dinner tonight."

They got into the truck and buckled their seat belts. It was a short trip back to the house, so they spent the time reliving the gymkhana events and admiring the prize belt buckle. By the time they got home and got the horses bathed and put away, it was almost dinnertime.

Ashleigh could tell her cousin was getting nervous. She didn't blame her. If Kaitlin's parents said no to running Ranger again, that would be the end of it. There would be no arguing. Ranger would be a saddle horse, and Kaitlin's dream would be crushed.

They ate outdoors again. This time Troy and his

father made fat, juicy cheeseburgers on the grill. The burgers were served with fresh garden greens and potato salad. Several times during the dinner Ashleigh tried to steer the conversation toward horse racing so that Kaitlin could work in her question about Ranger, but each time her cousin chickened out. Finally Jim brought up the subject, and there was no way Kaitlin could back out.

"How's Ranger's training going?" he asked. "Is he ready for life as a trail horse?"

Kaitlin hesitated, and Ashleigh kicked her hard under the table. She yelped and gave Ashleigh a nasty look.

"What is it, girls?" Linda said as she looked from one to the other.

Kaitlin took a big breath and began. "Ranger has really settled down during the past few weeks, ever since we started taking him out into the desert. He has really great stamina," she said. "Good enough to keep up with Ariel. There's that two-mile race coming up next week, and I really think Ranger could win it." She finished her speech and watched her parents' faces nervously.

Ashleigh crossed her fingers. Jim had a doubtful look on his face as he scratched his chin in contemplation.

"We could work him tomorrow morning," Troy said

quickly. "His time would tell us if there's been much of a change." Troy gave his sister an encouraging wink.

Kaitlin smiled at her brother in appreciation.

"I guess it couldn't hurt to try," Jim said. "That two-miler has a pretty decent purse on it. If Ranger can run a steady pace for the entire route, he'll wear them down."

"Yes!" Kaitlin cried as she jumped up and ran around the table to give her parents a hug. "Ranger will win that race! You'll see."

Linda tried to hide a smile. "Let's see if he makes it through the workout tomorrow before we put ourselves in the winner's circle."

Kaitlin sat down and snapped a crispy carrot between her teeth. "I believe in him," she said with pride. "Ranger is going to be the winner of that two-mile race!"

The next morning Ashleigh helped Kaitlin saddle Ranger for his work. "Here, let me do that," Ashleigh said as she pushed Kaitlin's fumbling hands away from the girth. "You're shaking like a tree in a windstorm."

Kaitlin crammed her hands into her pockets. "I'm just so nervous," she said. "This is Ranger's last chance. If he blows this and takes off through the sagebrush, then that's it. My parents will sell him for sure."

Ashleigh checked all the tack to make sure everything was perfect. "He'll be fine, Kate. Just you wait and see."

The rest of the family arrived at the barn. Troy put on his riding helmet, but Ashleigh noticed that he left his whip lying where it was. She smiled. Troy was on their side. He'd do his best with Ranger that morning.

Jim pulled his stopwatch out of his pocket. "Bring that beast on out here. Let's get this done."

Kaitlin's hands shook as she took Ranger's reins. The bay gelding snorted and looked at her with his big brown eyes.

"It's okay, boy," Kaitlin said, giving him a reassuring kiss on the muzzle.

Ranger blew through his lips and followed Kaitlin out of the barn. Jim legged Troy up, and they all followed them to the training oval.

"I can't sit," Kaitlin said as she paced nervously.

Linda gave her a big hug. "Look, honey." She pointed to where Ranger was backtracking with Troy. "Ranger's not playing around the way he normally does. I think he's going to do fine."

They watched as Troy turned the gelding the correct way of the track, trotted him off, then broke into a canter. Ranger bobbed his head a few times, then leaned into the bit and pricked his ears, galloping with energy.

"He looks good," Jim said as he waited for the pair to circle the track and come back to the half-mile pole for the workout.

As they approached the pole, Troy asked Ranger to stride out to a working speed. The colt pinned his ears and stretched his legs.

Jim kept watch on the clock. "It's not a blazing speed, but it could be good enough to run in the two-miler if he can keep it up. Let's hope Ranger doesn't take a detour through the desert this time."

Kaitlin and Ashleigh kept their fingers crossed as Ranger and Troy approached the area where the gelding had last made his rampage into the sagebrush.

Ranger breezed past the spot and continued on at a steady pace. As the pair came to the finish line, Jim signaled for them to go around again. Troy had a questioning look on his face, but he settled back down over the horse's withers and kept Ranger going at the same pace.

This time when they came to the finish line, Jim signaled for Troy to pull the horse up, but Ranger ran another half lap before he slowed.

Ranger pranced off the track with his head held high.

"He wanted to keep running," Troy said as he took his feet out of the irons and unknotted his reins.

Jim held up the stopwatch. "I clocked Ranger for the

entire mile and a quarter," he said with a smile. "Like I said before, he doesn't have much speed, but if he can run a steady pace for the entire two miles, I think he might have a chance."

Kaitlin's brows rose. "Does that mean you're going to give him a chance?"

Linda took Kaitlin by the shoulders and looked her square in the eye. "You and Ashleigh have done a lot of work with Ranger over the past several weeks. It's very obvious," she said. "But we all know that unless Ranger's times improve, he might not ever be able to run in the normal distance races. What are your hopes for Ranger, Kaitlin?"

Kaitlin shoved her hands deep into her pockets and kicked at the sand beneath her boots.

Ashleigh wanted to scream as the moments stretched out and Kaitlin still didn't answer. *Come on, Kate,* she willed silently. Finally, when she couldn't stand it anymore, Ashleigh gave her cousin a poke in the back. That got Kaitlin started.

"The first thing," Kaitlin began, "is the two-mile race. After that, maybe if Ranger trains more, he'll get better and run faster times, and then we can keep him in the stable."

"And if he doesn't?" Linda asked.

Kaitlin shrugged. "Tony's getting pretty old, and I can't keep borrowing your horse," she said. "If Ranger can win the two-miler, it would pay for his feed for the entire year. I thought maybe I could keep him as a replacement for Tony and use him as a saddle horse. Then once a year we could race him in the two-mile race."

Ashleigh secretly applauded her cousin. It had taken a lot of guts for her cousin to ask her parents for this. Now she, Kaitlin, and Troy all waited to hear the decision.

Jim patted Ranger's sweaty neck. "Sounds like a plan that could work. Let's get this horse cleaned up and fed. He's got a big race to run next week!"

Kaitlin turned to Ashleigh and slapped her a high five. "Thanks, Ash. I couldn't have done it without you."

Ashleigh followed her cousins back to the barn, feeling very pleased about the way things had turned out. She had so desperately wanted to return to Edgardale, but now she knew she had done the right thing by staying. Kaitlin had worked hard with Ranger. They both deserved a chance. But they weren't finished yet. The biggest challenge lay ahead. They had a week of hard work ahead of them before the big race. For now, the future winner of the two-mile race needed his bath.

• • •

"I can't believe we're here!" Kaitlin said as they turned Ranger loose in the receiving stall at the Lone Pine racetrack. "I don't think I can sit through all of those other races waiting for Ranger's race."

Ashleigh gave Ranger a small drink of water. The rest of the water would be withheld until after the race to make sure that he didn't bloat up and get a belly-ache. She laughed at Kaitlin's statement. "I don't think you're going to have much of a choice. The two-miler is the last race of the day. They're only running the fourth race right now."

Jim was making sure they had all of Ranger's equipment. "I've got to take the truck and trailer back to the parking lot," he said. "I'll meet everyone at the track kitchen in a few minutes."

Ashleigh and Kaitlin brushed the gelding and picked out his feet, then snapped the muzzle onto his halter to make sure he didn't fill up on hay before the race.

"We'll be back," Kaitlin told Ranger as they walked from the stall. "I don't know if I can eat anything," she said to Ashleigh as they joined Kaitlin's mom and brother for the walk to the track's cafeteria.

"You can split a plate of fries with me," Ashleigh suggested. "I'm still pretty full from breakfast and all the snacks we ate on the way here."

Jim had a table waiting for them when they got

there. They ordered and sat down to wait for their meal. When it arrived, they ate quickly so that they could watch a few of the other races before getting Ranger ready for his big start.

"It looks like Ranger is going off at pretty high odds," Troy said as he passed Kaitlin the racing program. "They don't think he can do it."

Ashleigh grinned. "There're going to be a lot of surprised bettors when the race is over."

They entered the trainers' stands on the backside of the racetrack. Ashleigh couldn't help but smile as she compared it to Keeneland and Churchill Downs. The trainers' stands at those big tracks were more luxurious than the main grandstand at Lone Pine.

Ashleigh sat on the wooden bench and looked out over the track. The racetracks in Kentucky had beautiful flowers, shrubs, and lakes. Lone Pine had a few trees and several pens that contained cows. "Why are there cows in the middle of the racetrack?" Ashleigh asked. "Doesn't that spook the horses?"

"The inside of the track doubles as a roping arena during the off season," Kaitlin explained. "Sometimes the horses get a little spooked when they hear the mooing. But if they've raced here before, they get used to it."

They watched several races and then returned to the receiving barn to ready Ranger for the race. Kaitlin pulled out a bunch of blue carnations that she had kept hidden in a cooler.

"He's going to be the prettiest horse in the race," Kaitlin said as she gathered the scissors and yarn.

Troy frowned. "Yuck! He's going to look like a sissy."

Kaitlin placed her hands on her hips and stuck out her tongue at her brother. "I want Ranger to look good for the win photo," she said as she removed his muzzle before tying him to the wall.

Ashleigh grabbed the mane-and-tail comb and began the preparation for placing the pretty blue flowers in Ranger's black mane. The little gelding fussed and bobbed his head as Ashleigh braided the flowers into his hair. "Hey!" she cried when the antsy horse reached around and tried to eat one of the flowers.

They finished the job just as the first call for the last race blared over the speaker system.

Kaitlin grabbed Ashleigh's arm. "This is it, Ash!" She ran around the stall, picking up buckets and rub rags, looking for the drench gun.

"Calm down," Ashleigh said as she handed the drench gun to Kaitlin and held Ranger's head so that his mouth could be washed with fresh water.

Kaitlin laughed. "Maybe it would be better if I let you guys do this. I'm too nervous, and Ranger is picking up on it."

Troy entered the stall with the bridle. "Let me and

Dad handle this," he said. "You two head on over to the front side. We'll meet you over there."

They walked to the front side of the racetrack and waited outside the saddling ring. There were many oohs and ahhs as Ranger was led into the ring.

"He looks great, girls," Linda said with pride. "Ranger is definitely the best-dressed horse in the race."

Ranger waited quietly while he was saddled, but he started dancing nervously when he was walked around the ring. He skittered sideways as the jockey mounted up, and chomped at the bit constantly.

"He looks scared," Kaitlin said. "I hope he's not too nervous to run."

Ashleigh found them a place along the track's rail and settled into her spot. "At least he looks like he knows what's happening this time," she said encouragingly. "The last two times he ran, he was just out here to play."

Ranger trotted past in the post parade, prancing sideways and kicking up his heels. His jockey pulled on the reins, trying to get the horse to line out.

Kaitlin rubbed her stomach. "I'm getting a bad feeling about this, Ash."

Ashleigh looped her arm through Kaitlin's. "He'll be okay," she assured her cousin. "Ranger is just working out some nervous energy before the race. Lots of horses do that."

The horses finished the post parade and cantered to the backside. The gate was stationed on the other side of the six-furlong track. The horses would pass the finish line three times before the race was over.

Kaitlin tightened her grip on Ashleigh's arm. "They're loading them into the gate."

They waited while all eight horses were led into the starting gate. There was a loud banging from the gate, and they could see the entire gate shake. Several of the gate crew converged on one stall.

"Bold Ranger is delaying the start," the announcer called. "It looks like they're all settled now. . . . And they're off for the running of this year's two-mile spectacular!"

"Oh, no!" Kaitlin cried as Ranger broke dead last from the starting gate. "That's the same thing he did last time."

They watched helplessly as Ranger settled into his stride many lengths behind the last horse. The Thoroughbreds passed the finish line the first time with the eight horses spread out over quite a distance. Ranger ran his steady pace at least thirty lengths behind the first-place horse.

Ashleigh tried to ignore the snickers and rude comments she heard coming from the crowd as Ranger loped past them.

A short, dark-haired man with a fat cigar laughed

161

and slapped his leg as Ranger passed. "I bet that first-place horse laps Bold Ranger by the end of the race," he cried.

"Don't pay any attention to them," Ashleigh said. "We've still got a mile and a half to go."

As the horses came down the stretch for the second time, the leaders began to fade, and other horses moved up to take their places.

"Rowdy Dan moves into the lead with Bright Star running second and Truly Yours in third," the announcer called. "Bold Ranger is in the rear, running easily."

"Come on, Ranger!" Kaitlin hollered as the little bay galloped past on the inside rail. But Ranger continued his steady pace, still running far behind the next-to-last horse.

"He looks like he's starting to close the gap," Troy said as the horses entered the turn, beginning their final lap of the course.

Ashleigh scrunched her lips. Once again she wasn't sure if Ranger was picking up speed or if the others were just dropping back. But as they ran up the backside of the track Ranger began to make a move.

"Look, Kaitlin," Ashleigh said as she pulled her cousin's hands from her eyes. "Ranger is moving up! He just passed a horse!"

The announcer's voice boomed over the speaker

system. "Bright Star takes the lead as Rowdy Dan drops back and Truly Yours moves into second place. Bold Ranger is making his move on the last turn, running wide to pass the fading horses on the rail."

"Go, Ranger!" Ashleigh and the Gilberts screamed as the bay gelding went wide around the turn, passing horses as he went. He pounded down the homestretch with his ears plastered against his head, his legs working like pistons as he passed another horse.

"Bold Ranger makes his move on the outside of the racetrack!" the announcer hollered excitedly as the crowd went wild. "He's passed Truly Yours and has set his sights on Bright Star!"

Ashleigh and Kaitlin jumped up and down, pounding on the rail as the roar of the crowd drowned out their voices. Ranger caught Bright Star at the sixteenth pole and hung there for a moment, running neck and neck with the larger Thoroughbred.

"Don't stop now!" Kaitlin cried. "You've got only a few more strides to go. Come on, Ranger, run!"

As if he heard her call, Ranger pulled ahead of the lead horse by a nose, then stretched it out to a neck. He crossed the finish line just three-quarters of a length ahead of the other horse.

"He did it!" Kaitlin hollered as she hugged everyone standing near her. "He won the two-miler!"

Jim herded the family toward the winner's circle.

"You and Ashleigh go catch your horse and bring him into the circle," he said. "We'll put on our best smiles for the win photo."

Ashleigh hugged Kaitlin as they waited for Ranger to return and the track stewards to post the race as official. Ranger trotted back with his jockey smiling happily.

"I wasn't sure he had it in him," the jockey said with a grin as he stood in the stirrups so his valet could remove the outer girth for the win photo. "But this colt had a ton of energy left at the end of the race. I wish they ran this two-miler at some of the other tracks!"

Kaitlin led Ranger into the winner's circle.

"Here you go, Kate," her father said as he handed her a piece of paper.

"What's this?" Kaitlin asked in surprise as she tried to keep Ranger from eating the cream-colored sheet.

Ashleigh recognized the blue-lined Thoroughbred registration papers, but she kept quiet, not wanting to spoil the surprise.

"It's Ranger's registration papers," Linda said. "He's officially yours to keep."

Kaitlin hugged each of her parents and then pulled Ashleigh to stand beside her at Ranger's head for the win photo. "You're as much responsible for Ranger's win as I am," she said proudly. "We wouldn't be here without you."

The track photographer raised his camera. "Everyone smile!"

Ashleigh smiled so hard, her cheeks hurt. Her mission here was finished. She'd had a great vacation, and she'd helped her cousin accomplish her dream. In just a few short days she would be on her way home to Edgardale to capture her own dream. Stardust and her coming foal were waiting!

CHRIS PLATT rode her first pony when she was two years old and hasn't been without a horse since. Chris spent five years at racetracks throughout Oregon working as an exercise rider, jockey, and assistant trainer. She currently lives in Reno, Nevada, with her husband, Brad, five horses, three cats, a llama, a potbellied pig, and a parrot. Between writing books, Chris rides endurance horses for a living and drives draft horses for fun in her spare time.